A Moth in the Flames

Book Five in 'The Kingdom of Durundal' series

S.E. Turner

Copyright S. E. Turner 2018

The right of S. E. Turner to be identified as the author of this work has been asserted by her in accordance with the Copyright, Designs and Patents Act 1988.

ACKNOWLEDGMENTS

Jamie Flack.

Daisy Jane.

Nancy Stopper.

Jeremy Boughtwood.

My friends and family for their enthusiasm and encouragement.

My three daughters who continue to inspire me.

BY S.E. TURNER

The Kingdom of Durundal Series

Book One: *A Hare in the Wilderness*
Book Two: *A Wolf in the Dark*
Book Three: *A Leopard in the Mist*
Book Four: *A Stag in the Shadows*
Book Five: *A Moth in the Flames*

www.kingdomofdurundal.com

'Whatever you read now you must believe. I will tell you things that seem impossible and highly improbable. But remember that we live in a world where everything is decided by what we can see and what we touch. If we can't see it or we don't understand it, then we perceive that it doesn't exist. But it does exist, and what may seem impossible here, is in fact highly probable in another world.'

'We are all connected.'

To Rachel
Congrahulations! You've read the complete series
Now to the next one
B. Turner

PROLOGUE

THE MORNING AIR was dark with the smell of rain, and the dragons peered out from their stone surroundings as if they were looking directly at Cornelius. A cloud seemed to hang over him today, ragged and black as his cloak. He paced about restlessly, muttering to himself, and the crenel of witches trembled when he brushed past them. He was agitated about something—he did not know what. He just knew that he needed a change. After three years of living in the cave, something had to change.

Outside, waves crashed against the jagged rocks, eager to get past the entrance of the cave's mouth. The wind picked up its pace and threaded its way through the canyon into the dome of gargoyles where it curled round the hundred faces and breathed energy into them. The fire glowed with the life-giving elements and rose higher, burning brighter with every passing minute. He caught his breath for a moment, unsure of what was happening. He heard a rustling, and then an even fiercer light bloomed.

He shielded his eyes and felt his breath caught in his throat. One hand gripped his neck and the other protected him from the glare. The roar of power settled down, and then went pitch black.

'What witchcraft is this?' his voice quivered.

All he could hear was the sound of his own breathing: loud, anxious, agitated. He calmed himself. The light returned, and out of the flames stepped a life form. He didn't know what it was. He backed away, stumbling, slipping, falling. Hot coals ignited the being. The black charcoaled image stood there burning, as ashes around its feet lifted in a frenzy and swirled around the body before disappearing into the orifice of a throat. The blackened skin became young and even skin-toned. Long golden hair grew from the crown of the head. Though shrouded in a fine gossamer, the face was beautiful, and the body was perfect. A naked woman stood before him veiled in plumes of smoke. Fiery amber eyes pierced his own and didn't stray from their focus.

'Cornelius, I have watched you grow into a man. I have seen the change in you. But I know you are about to leave this place and embark on a journey.'

Cornelius pinched himself. He shook his head, not quite believing what was in front of him or what he had just heard.

'You are not the frightened little boy anymore. You are strong, and you are courageous. I can help you become even stronger.'

'How?' his voice was small and weak.

'The gods of darkness protect you and I can give you immortality.'

Cornelius laughed out loud.

The fire soared, the wind howled, and the amber eyes glared. 'Do not mock me!' She bellowed.

He swallowed the laugh and spoke quietly. 'Why would you do that for me?'

'Because I want something in return.'

He braced himself, fearful of what she would request from him.

'What can I give you?' He heard the whisper.

Her eyes burned brighter, the plumes of smoke clung to her curves. The breeze curled around his torso.

Her gaze bore into his very soul.

He turned away.

'Look at me Cornelius.'

Their eyes met.

'It is written that a warrior will charge through the kingdoms and seek vengeance for those whom have been slain and tortured. This warrior will be born from the seed of the living and the womb of the dead.'

He dropped his head sideways in astonishment.

'Her name will be Sansara, and her purpose will be to bring peace. She will be able to take many forms, but in this life, it will be of a human.'

His rhetoric was mocking. 'That is impossible. There is too much evil out there for one person to take care of. Even a ten thousand strong army of powerful bowmen and a well-established cavalry cannot do what you propose'

The fire blinded him. The wind froze him to the spot.

He frowned.

'I want you to father that child... with me.'

. . .

She saw the pink cavern of his mouth.

'If you do this for me, then I give you my word: no ordinary man will take your life.'

'How do I know you are speaking the truth?'

The fire roared again, the waves snarled foam around the cavern, and the wind raced through the gloom.

'How can you take care of a child? What will you do? Where will you go?' He continued, despite the wrath.

'That is not your concern. The child will be mine and given everything she needs, I can assure you of that.' Her voice grew thin 'But I grow weak in this life form... I am tiring... now do we have a bargain?'

CHAPTER ONE

Travellers used to speak of an island, unknown to many, that was kept hidden from the outside world for thousands of years. Ships would pass its sandy shores, but few would ever stop there, for the island offered nothing for them.

The inhabitants lived in scattered pods around the island. It was said that these people could talk with animals, make spells, summon storms, and make men think they could fly. Seafarers kept well away from this place, expecting lightning bolts to come down from the sky like shards and incinerate them on the spot.

But one ship load of looters did not heed the warnings and launched an attack on the peaceful community, desecrating monuments, destroying artefacts, and burning scriptures. Worshippers were hacked down as they prayed in the sacred lake. Others were cut down as they worked the land. They screamed and raised their hands in defence. Some pleaded, many tried to lay curses, but the result was the same. After the slaughter, all surviving animals were rounded up, the village was set alight, and the men urinated in the sacred water. They say the sea ran red for months, the rain fell like tears, and the winds never stopped howling. When the ship set sail again, it ran aground in the storms, and all on board were lost to the sea.

For years the island lay empty, fragile, barely breathing.

Now, the birds have begun to sing once again, and an old woman lives there with her three daughters. She is easily recognisable because of her long woollen robe. She walks barefooted. Her grey hair ends at her waist, her face is slightly wrinkled, yet her body is lithe and firm. Her three daughters are beautiful: tall and sculpted. The very epitome of a goddess. They have smooth olive skin, their hair is plaited with delicate orchids, they speak with the wind, and are told things by the elements.

They see cruelty spreading, and they see cities burning and people running. They see the hatred in young men's hearts and know the killing will go on until the winds can change things. They hear a girl calling to them, a boy cries out for help, and a mother weeps for her dead baby. They feel their anger, their weakness, their danger. The old woman talks to the storms and sends them with full force to eradicate the poison. The gale tries desperately to swallow the evil, to clean the slate and pave the way for love and light. But all it does is delay things for a while, and the hatred and the burning and the running continues.

The women don't like intrusion, and they don't like visitors, until the day the wind tells them of a change—

bad things will happen to those who come to their island uninvited.

Apart from the giant, that is.

Once a year, when the weather is warm and the conditions are right, a giant oval emerges from the ocean and its wet flippers soon become covered in pebbled sand. Slowly, the hulking sea beast pulls herself up the beach's crest—she is not used to handling a four-hundred-pound frame on dry land. She is accustomed to the protection from the women, though, and she drags herself up on to the beach. Once in a safe place, she begins to dig deeper and deeper into the sand. Soon a massive hole is dug out, and this gentle sea creature begins to lay her eggs. When the duty is done, she covers the precious cargo and lumbers back towards the sea—into the quiet depths, into the safety of her vast home.

On Mawi's Island, many have met their doom already, a few have survived and cannot speak of what they have seen, but the crone is ready for anything. She has nurtured her brood. She has watched her hatchlings grow. The island will never fall again. For this woman is a sorceress of the highest order: a witch, an immortal being who has born three daughters from mortals—men chosen for their courage and virtue, for their integrity and strength. One of these men has fallen to the sword, another has fallen to the ocean. The crone did not choose well.

But one survives.

Now it is time.

CHAPTER TWO

SANSARA WAS DREAMING. She was walking naked down a long secret passage, a winding tunnel of dampness and fragility tinged with the scent of rose petals and jasmine. She followed the aroma through the dark twisted maze until she found herself descending a narrow set of marble stairs hemmed with an intricately carved bronze rail. The staircase swooped downwards and still the scent was leading her into the eternal abyss—an everlasting decent. At the foot of the stairs were three doors. One was oak, one was ruby, and one was lapis lazuli. Unknowing which one to choose, she reached out intuitively and turned the old gnarled knocker before opening the wooden door. It creaked and groaned, unwilling to share its secrets. She didn't know what to expect, and the endless minutes ticked by like a recurring nightmare. The room was musty, and a small beam of light fell on a richly decorated granite tomb. On the top, a man and a woman lay next to each other. They both held swords to their breasts, and they both wore crowns. She noticed the relief of a hare and a stag on the side of the coffin alongside some names that she couldn't decipher. Sansara trembled as she ran a finger across the woman's smooth porcelain face. She imagined she saw her take a sharp intake of breath when she felt a line carved into her cheek. Sansara recoiled instantly and her gaze fell on the man at her side. A trickle of red blood ran from an arrow wound in his heart. The weapon was still protruding, the blood collected in whirlpools at the base of the tomb and towards her feet. She wanted to run but her legs wouldn't move. She wanted to scream but nothing came out. The aqueous liquid continued to form blood-red petals that merged together as blooms, and a chaos held her suspended as she tried to break free from the suffocating mire. In the distance, voices and shuffling footsteps were getting nearer. She became confused and disorientated. Fear gripped her.

HER SISTER TOUCHED her arm gently. 'Sansara, wake up. You are having another nightmare.'

Sansara flared her eyes wide open and heard herself panting. She looked around, glad of the kind face and familiar voice. Steadying her own, she took hold of her younger sibling's hand.

'Are you okay, Sansara? You were thrashing about a lot more this time.'

'I'm sorry. I didn't mean to frighten you.' Her voice was sincere.

Ellis cradled Sansara tenderly and brushed away the tears.

'I keep having the same dream, every night it's the same, and every time I am held in a state of panic as I cannot move.'

'I know this dream is a burden, I know you are in turmoil. But know that you are safe—you are always safe with us.

A wisp of hair fell onto her cheek.

Her elder sister came over and sat on the edge of the bed. 'You must talk to mother. She will know what it means.' Phoebe pushed the hair from her face and wrapped it behind the back of her ear.

Sansara dabbed the tears with the back of her hand and sniffed back a runny nose. 'Yes, I must. I will do that this very day.'

THE MOST USED room on Mawi's Island was the kitchen filled with sounds and smells that contributed to a feeling of love and security. This kitchen was huge, with low beams over a floor of polished driftwood tiles. It had ovens and kettles and huge pots and pans, with ladles and serving spoons as big as plates. As a small child, Sansara and her sisters watched as their mother kneaded the bread dough with strong firm knuckles and diced up vegetables with a long, curved knife. Best of all was when mother made honey cakes and lemon biscuits and the girls would scoff them all with huge mugs of dandelion tea. Herbs and plants would be brewed and fermented to ward off evil spirits and bring continued peace to their solitary island. The girls would sit at one end of the long heavy worktable watching their mother work her magic and chant ancient words. Mawi knew by smell, taste, or a simple touch when each potion was just right and stored them in jars and vials and earthenware pots. There was a certain divination about her, a knowledge and power that surpassed any mortal being. She was tall, with long grey hair turning white at the crown, and speckled flecks that glistened by the firelight and shone in the sun. Sansara loved those strands, for they looked like silver raindrops that changed every day, and when her mother kissed her goodnight, she could always see another silver strand that rewarded her mother's higher instinct and exceptional skills.

Outside lay an arrangement of sheds and barns and hen roosts and dovecotes. A small coal pit was in the centre of the yard surrounded by the smell of heather and a green scent of pine drifting over the hills.

By the time Sansara was ten years old, she knew the medicinal content of every single plant. She could identify those which could heal wounds, those which could cure ailments, and those which could kill pain. She knew the poisonous ones, the ones that could cause a mere tummy upset, and those that could be fatal.

Her favourite memories were when mother took them out for the day... into the meadows burgeoning with life.

'I want to find lots of plants today, especially spinach and radishes, because they calm inflammations and viral infections. We have run low on those, so I need you to get some for me.'

Nimble fingers and keen noses sought out the hidden apothecary amongst the vegetation, naked to the ordinary eye but a life support to the ardent explorer. And as if conjured up by magic, a blanket of herbaceous flowers waved their vibrant blooms urgently in the south westerly breeze.

'Which plants heal?' asked Ellis, running ahead, hungry for knowledge and new skills.

'Yarrow is the most valuable healing remedy, and we need a lot of those, so look for its feathery leaves, strong stems and broad white flower heads.'

'What is this one?' asked Phoebe, foraging amongst the stalks and colours.

'That's oregano. It's a very good aid against poisonous insect bites. And this one is thyme which is excellent for tummy aches.'

The barrage of questions continued from Sansara. 'What about these pretty yellow flowers?'

'Those are marigolds that can heal skin wounds, burns, and eye inflammation. And this is mint which is very good for digestion.'

But they also knew the effects of aconitum, of hellebore, of white snakeroot and wild iris. Of blanket weed and laburnum, for these were some of the most powerful plants, and a simple concoction was always close to hand.

A CHILL SLICED the air that morning. The doves cooed outside and the rooster heralded the start of the day. Sansara came downstairs, carrying a heavy heart and a weight on her shoulders. Her sisters watched as she went into the kitchen, and when they saw she had not changed her mind, they each took a bucket of grain to feed the chickens and doves.

'Mother, I really need to talk with you about something.'

'Yes, I know—I have been waiting for this day to arrive.'

'You have?'

'I have. But come sit here with me for a while. I have baked some fresh bread and made you a cup of dandelion tea.'

Sansara sat beside Mawi and sipped slowly from the tea, though she never once averted her gaze. Her mother looked at her green eyes hemmed with long lashes, and the soft ebony tendrils hanging loose around her face. She saw that her high cheekbones still carried the flesh of youth, and yet her firm body told her she was very much a woman now. Mawi stroked her hand tenderly. 'I know you have seen things in a dream.'

Sansara gulped slowly. *How could she know?*

'I know of your turmoil and uncertainty.'

'Mother, how do you know?' The burning question escaped her pursed lips like a spell.

Mawi sat back with closed eyes and breathed in the air, her chest seemed to rattle, her bones creaked.

'How old do you think I am, Sansara?'

'You are my mother, you can only be about a score and ten.'

Mawi cackled and her chest rattled again. 'I am seven hundred years old.'

Sansara choked back her tea. 'What? Mother, please

don't play jokes on me while my mind is in turmoil. I was hoping for answers, not untruths."

'I am telling you the truth. I am seven hundred years old—maybe even a bit older.'

'But that's impossible.' Sansara put down the cup.

'Is it?' said Mawi. 'How old are you then?'

'Sixteen. You know that I am.'

'And in sixteen years you've learned about everything that is possible and impossible?'

Sansara felt the blush. 'But you are my mother, and I would know if you were that ancient.'

'But I am ancient, Sansara. Look at me. I have a croaky voice, I am stooped and withered, my chest rattles, and I hold an old gnarled staff to walk with. Of course I am ancient.'

'But not seven hundred years old, Mother. No one is seven hundred years old.'

Her mother peered at her through a dipped expression and sighed heavily. 'I have to tell you that we live in a world where everything is decided by what we can see and touch. If we can't see it or we don't understand it, then it doesn't exist.'

'Mother, please. Stop playing games with me.'

'What if I told you that what may seem impossible here, is in fact highly probable in another world.'

Sansara frowned at her again.

'And quite possibly, that other world might choose you to do something that has to be done.'

'Me?'

'Yes, you Sansara. You have been chosen by a higher force to go on a journey.'

'Why?' Her voice was incredulous.

'I made a pact with a mortal man... your father. Though only a few years ago in his world, in my world, it was many years ago. You age as I want you to age.'

'I don't understand, Mother, really I don't.'

Mawi sighed. 'I am a witch, a sorceress, a maker of magic. I chose a man who would father me a strong daughter. I wanted that child to have the mortal energy of a human, but the energy of a witch.'

'Why?'

'So that you could choose immortality over mortality. So that you could make a difference. So that you could bring about change. I have seen such horrors, such suffering, so many lives ruined and cut down without reason. I want you to make that difference, to make that change, to ease the suffering that has gone before.'

Sansara shook her head from side to side. 'How will I do that, Mother. How on earth will I do that?'

'Your father said the same thing.' Mawi looked into the flames flickering in the hearth.

'Well, he was right.' Sansara sighed and looked to the floor.

Mawi lifted her chin and, for the first time, Sansara looked deep into a pair of ageing eyes that had seen more of the world than she cared for.

'There is an island a few days sail from here, it is called Tarragon Island. It has everything for you on there: all the plants that you need, and all the herbs that you will require. It is fertile land. You will grow there like the mighty oak grows from a tiny seed—an acorn which is full of nature, knowledge and truth. Sansara, as you spread your wings, you will grow like you never thought possible. You will find your power. You will rise up like the mighty oak.'

Sansara shook her head, still not convinced. 'What if I don't want to?'

'But you must. It is written.'

'Why can't you do it? You have experience. You have it engrained in you.'

Mawi sighed again. 'I am too old. I don't have the fight in me anymore. That's why I did what I did, to secure the future and to pass this challenge on.'

Sansara shook her head and chewed on the corner of her mouth. Never in her wildest imagination had she seen herself doing something like this.

'Why can't Ellis or Phoebe come with me? Why do I have to do it alone?' Her tone was pleading.

'Because it is written by a higher force than me—the Fates. It is your destiny. I can see your father. I can hear him calling. I couldn't see the others. It has to be you and you alone.'

Sansara moved to the window.

'Mother, please don't make me do this. I will miss the sound of the boar, the flight of the crow, and the bobbing tails of the rabbits. They are my friends; you and my sisters are all I need. Please don't make me do this.' She dipped her head as she reflected. 'Do you remember the first day we were here and I was strapped to your back, and we disturbed the female boar with her brood of piglets.'

'Yes, I remember it well,' The old crone opened up

the embryonic memories that were stored in her tired old mind.

> They were walking through dense undergrowth. Sansara was secured tightly onto her mother's back with a sling. She was asleep while the sorceress foraged and selected the ripest berries by putting them into her bag. She used her hands to hack away the bracken and vegetation obscuring her path. She hadn't realised how far she had gone into the thicket, and it was there that she heard an unusual sound. Her ears tuned in to a disturbing grunting and snorting which seemed to be coming towards her. She stopped moving and hardly dared to breathe. She felt the child on her back. She would be safe there, she decided. The sorceress had to stay put. She couldn't reach her gnarled staff to magic it away, nor did she have any herbs that would make a spell. She couldn't turn and run, because then her child would get the full force should the creature decide to attack. She had no choice but to wait it out as rigid as she could until the animal passed. The sounds of snapping branches and moving bushes got closer, and the muffled snorts of something feasting was perilously near. She had her dagger ready and crouched down low. The waiting was intolerable, and she tried to calm her pulsating heart and rapid breathing. The beaded sweat of fear ran down her face, and despite the urge to wipe it away, she stood perfectly still.
>
> But Sansara moved behind her; and suddenly,

without warning, the animal burst through the thick growth. Its large powerful body was supported by short stocky legs, and wickedly sharp lower canines protruded like tusks along both sides of its snout. Small deep set eyes on a massive head were wild, and it was storming towards her with the full wrath of a tempestuous tornado. As it got closer, the smell was nauseating. The hairs bristled over a grey humped back, and the skin was cracked with ground in mud and faeces.

Strangely, and without hesitation, the animal stopped when it saw the mother and child. It stamped its small feet and snorted, raising its huge head into the air. It sniffed the human forms as if processing the danger, then lowered its jaw. Minutes later, a brood of youngsters collected round her and she trotted off into the distance. She knew these beings were not a threat to her. She knew that her family were still safe on the island.

Sansara's mother returned to the present and tried to explain. 'I remember, my child. But you have come to this island for a reason, just as I brought Ellis and Phoebe to this place. But with their father's demise through weakness, you are the one with added strength. Like a moth that has been protected in a cocoon, you must now spread your wings and fly. You have to do this. It is your destiny and why I brought you here.'

'I am only sixteen years old, Mother. How will I survive?' Sansara turned to face her mother. *How could you send a child out into the wilderness?*

'I have already taught you how to live off the land. You already know many spells and lots of magic. But you will also have my staff.' She pointed to the old gnarled stick in the corner. 'That will protect you. But use it wisely. Inexperienced hands will drain the power. Once you have become a master, you can use it at will. Though, believe me, with the amount of power that you will summon, you won't need the wand very often.'

'And the people in my dream. Who are they?'

'They are your father and his sister. When he sired you, I gave him immortality, but warned him to beware of the stag, for the stag has the power to kill him. In his world, he has been slain by a man who carries the totem of the stag. It was not a deliberate action, but your father is dying. In his world, he is between lives. He is calling for you right now. You cannot hear him. You can only see him in your dreams, or what you are permitted to see. Only I can hear his cry. And only when you hold the Sapphire of the Sorceress will you be able to hear him. Then you can save his life.'

Sansara shot a withering look before her mother made another startling revelation.

'You have met him once before.'

The young girl frowned in disbelief. 'When?'

'Do you remember that day when the seafarers came to our shores?'

'I do. I remember it was chaos when the boat docked. We were all terrified.'

'Yes, I could see from their behaviour that things could turn sour.' Mawi's own expression paled with the memory. 'I remember watching them staggering onto the shore. The sand seemed to sway underfoot as they found their land legs again. But those same masses who descended onto our remote, quiet island were soon treating it as their home. No manners and no respect—as they so often do.'

Sansara shook her head as she remembered.

'Your father, Cornelius, was the young man perched on top of the cliff.'

'Yes, I vaguely remember him. But I only caught a momentary glimpse. I was more concerned about the others and what they could do.'

Mawi breathed heavily through her nose and nodded. 'My revenge was swift. Most of them perished on that fateful trip.'

Sansara wiped away a tear. 'And you want me to save this man?'

'It is written, my child.'

'Does he deserve it?'

'He must, otherwise we would not be called.'

Sansara felt the fatigue of hearing so much.

'I know you are tired, my child. I feel the heavy weight on your shoulders. I really do. But it is out of my hands. I am merely the messenger.'

Sansara smiled wearily.

But Mawi hadn't finished. 'There is one more thing I must share with you.'

Sansara lifted her eyes.

'Your father has harboured a dark secret for most of his life. He is now required to open it up like an old wound. What happened affected many people—too many people. He has to face the past again.'

Sansara raised an eyebrow.

Her mother continued. 'You have to relay that message to him.

'How long will it take me to learn my craft and send the message?'

'Many years will pass. Many obstacles will come your way, but they are all challenges sent from a higher force. You must pass the tests, then you will gain the knowledge.

'When do I go?'

'You leave now, Sansara, before the nightmares become stronger and claim you forever. You are permitted to take your bow and a sheath of arrows.'

'Anything else?'

'Only the clothes that you stand in.'

Sansara looked down at her long woollen robe. She reached for her worn grey cloak, hanging on the old familiar hook. She didn't want to say goodbye to her sisters. It would be too painful. She didn't want to say goodbye to her mother, either. But her mother probably knew that already, because she spoke her final words, 'Go now, daughter. Your vessel awaits. Destiny is written. It is up to you to act wisely.'

CHAPTER THREE

The tall mast swayed and the weathered decks creaked as the ship swayed in gentle swells. The grey sailcloth sighed and strained as the easterly breeze pushed her along—side to side, up and down. Endlessly.

Sansara saw nothing but sea and clouds interspersed with a few sunny spells and patches of rain. The sea gulls would fly alongside her but disappear quickly when they felt a change in the air. This gave her time to reflect on everything she had heard. It had been a lot to take in, she thought. But now with the stillness of time and the sun and moon for company , she began to piece together what was being asked of her.

On the third day, there were no gulls. She saw that a caravan of black clouds had piled up against each other, and by dusk, she could lightning flickered to the west, followed by the distant crash of thunder. As the sea grew rougher, the angry waves rose up like serpents to smash their heads against the hull, splitting the crest with such force that she struggled to keep the ship on course. This storm was big. The winds began to howl, forcing the ship high on its stern and then crashing down again. Anything that wasn't tightly secured was thrown to port and then back to the starboard over and over again. By the time the storm broke, morning was creeping over the horizon, the weather had settled, and the skies cleared. It was as though nothing had happened at all. The sea was calm and glistening again while small white clouds drifted nonchalantly by and the gulls had dutifully returned to escort her ship.

Once again, the great masts flapped with the effort, and gentle breezes helped the ship on its way. Sansara watched the sun bounce off the crystal waters beneath her and merge with the specks of grey on a distant skyline. She soon came to appreciate the sharp salty smell of the air, and the vastness of the horizon trimmed with a band of azure on a clear day while the sea remained a rich shade of cyan.

She began to speak to the gulls and sometimes wished she could fly alongside them—if only for a day, even an hour, maybe a minute—just to feel that sense of power and unrivalled freedom.

The beautiful azure sky turned black again, and the crystal cyan sea morphed into an angered silver-grey creature. As the wind howled off its back, the canvas snapped and cracked in response. Sansara reefed the sails again. The hull bellowed undeterred, and the crows-nest stood firm as it was blasted with several tonnes of spray.

The squall picked up pace and the decks below were getting soaked, but still Sansara stood tall. She gripped the rail at the bow of the ship and breathed in the voracious wind while the hammering rain beat down on her, leaving her soaked and windswept, but undeterred. *'You won't break me this soon, not yet, not while I still have fire in my body and a will to survive.'*

Day after day, the young woman stood on the deck, drinking in the scenery of the vast horizons where an endless sky and a menagerie of birds flew alongside the ship. On some occasions, she was lucky enough to see a whale breaching or a school of dolphins jumping to the tune of the waves. The early morning was the best time to see them—it seemed they, too, were excited by the rising sun. And after a long time brushing against the sea floor hidden in the depths, they would rise to the surface to take in the wondrous spectacle themselves. She had never seen that vision before, and because she thought she probably would never have the chance again, she stood at the bow most days, watching for a glimpse of the great mammals of the ocean.

The tall masts continued to sway, and the weathered decks creaked, and the battered ship made its way slowly to a remote bay that led to a wide stretch of land. It was dusk now. It was quiet. Only the sound of the lapping waves escorted her. This was her new home. The wind had brought her here. This is where should would live and learn her craft.

She dropped the anchor with a splash, and collecting a few essential items, took her small coracle to the shore. This idyllic tranquil beach led to a beautiful glade of palm trees where pods of stones and driftwood greeted her. She picked a path that would take her to a good elevated position, a place from whence she could see yet not be seen. Where the winds would bring forth news of inclement weather, or worse—an unwelcome visitor.

Finding her land legs again, she climbed over rocky crags, up steel grassy hillsides and into the tundra. She edged her way through a notch between the peaks where a soft hill was thick with grass and a breeze brought in a fresh scent of night. Below her stretched the hem of a forest and beyond that the open sea. A hazy mist glazed a beautiful turquoise lake, and the stones rolled green and smooth by river currents that hemmed the shoreline. This lake was full of lashing fish and would provide a staple diet to supplement the grouse that took flight. This would be a good vantage point. This is where she would make a home.

When the low sun spilled a fragile path for the moon, she began in earnest to gather dead leaves, dry moss and a few thin twigs to start the fire. These nights were still fairly cold, and it was the foolish traveller who left warmth and shelter to the last minute.

With her fire drill secure and the continual friction from her hands, she could soon smell the woodsmoke and saw the notch blacken. Then she saw a wisp of smoke. That vision fuelled her. Even though her palms were sore and her arms ached all over, she kept going. With more glows and more smoke, she held her head parallel to the hearth and began to blow on it. She watched it grow brighter with each breath she exhaled and die down as she inhaled. She added tiny bits of leaves with dry moss and continued to blow. Then a spark grew from out of the hearth which turned into a small flame. She blew harder, fed it more fuel. When it had taken hold, she added a few twigs, adding larger pieces of wood when it had established itself.

As she watched her man-made giant rise into the air, it ignited a dormant emotion in her—a surge like nothing she had ever known before. She felt its power, its ancient wisdom, its pure magic—the hypnotising effect that could lure a man into its core for warmth but send the most vicious predator running from the hungry serpent.

She cooked a freshly killed grouse over a small spit, took some much needed water from her flagon and whilst reminiscing about the past few days, she watched the sun pooling into a crimson horizon, filling her eyes with awe on a magnitude she would never get tired of seeing.

From her high elevation, she could see the magnificent mountain range, impassable to climb, but from a safe distance, her summits glimmered pink like long silk tongues. The foothills and the smaller peaks were lost in its shadows. Sansara felt equally small in its presence, but even though the sun had melted into the horizon now, the moon was casting a bright clear night, and the mountain range took on a completely new perspective.

'I hope I can succeed this task. I hope I don't let my mother down, or indeed my father, for he will die without me.' She took another swig of water. 'I will miss my sisters. I will miss my life there. I hope they fare well without me.' She looked up to the full moon coming into view. 'Can we all see the same moon?' she wondered. 'Or am I in a different world to everyone else, where time has no boundaries and the future is different for us all?' The conundrum tired her. She needed sleep, and finding a grassy mound to lean against, she thought about her sisters.

'Do you ever remember falling asleep?' she heard her younger sister saying. 'You never do because the night air is mysterious like that. It descends on you like a heavy shroud, its long black fingers slowly concealing everything in its path. Mist and darkness hover like a hideous veil, bewitching its prey and stripping it bare of energy and life.' She would dramatize her voice and curl her tongue around every word. 'Sneaking up and sucking the life from the victim who is unaware and unprepared. It's impossible to fight back the aroma and stifling effects of dusk and nightfall. Leaves shake and whisper to each other as the cold night air descends. Branches creak and crane, and twigs seem to snap unprovoked.' Wild, searching eyes added to the terrifying rendition. 'Who knows what goings on occur under this engulfing spell. Who knows what tricks are played and acted out when the eyelids drop so heavily over tired eyes. Who knows what demons come out to play under the blanket of the night?' The voice in her tired head trailed off and she succumbed to the pull of the night.

THE LONG HOURS of sleep gritted her eyes as she watched her surroundings brighten into the start of another day. The pit was still smouldering contentedly, and it made her stomach rumble as she thought of food.

She eased herself up on to her elbow at the thought of doing a little exploring and poured herself a cup of water, adding a portion of the moly that she had brought with her. The generous mix of herbs sank into the cold water as one lump then bobbed up to the surface, bursting into dry powder. She gulped down the lumpy concoction in one bitter mouthful. Levering herself up, she grabbed her pitcher and made her way towards the lake.

A MIST HAD SETTLED round the dense forest and weaved its way round the massive oaks. In the distance, a few twigs snapped, some leaves rustled, but she wasn't deterred. It was just the creatures of the forest foraging for food, she decided. She took a winding path down to the left and saw the lake shimmering as though all the stars had fallen from the sky the night before. She couldn't remember the last time she had bathed—so much had happened recently, But the ebb and flow murmured quietly and begged her to enter. Disrobing cautiously, she felt the need to look around, but after determining she was alone, she stepped into the crystal clear shallows.

The cool water felt so good against her naked skin. It had been such a long time since she had ventured into such calm ripples. She waded in slowly, carefully gripping the slimy base with her toes, and felt the silt ooze between them. She giggled with the thrill. A few small fish were brave enough to nibble her submerged feet, and she gasped with the surprise. She splashed herself gently and washed her face. The grime and sweat rolled off with each shower, and then she submerged in the water and let it spill over her entire body. She stayed there, experiencing the magical moment, as the enormous trees tilted towards her.

A flock of birds flew gracefully overhead. She stood up to embrace the morning and held her arms out wide. She held her gaze to the morning sky, squeezed the excess water from her hair, and thanked the gods that she had made it to the island.

Back at her camp, she feasted on birds' eggs for breakfast, and taking water from her recently filled flagon, she began to hear more sounds of the dawn.

Here, the flowers were thick along the pastures edge and buzzed with the sound of bees. Spiders, crickets and beetles jostled for position in the miniature ground level fortress, and a range of different pollinators darted along its vibrant hem. She nodded approvingly at her choice of home, and began the exhausting process of collecting stones, chopping wood and making clay to hold it all together.

Remembering her mother's instructions, she didn't want to use the wand for fear of draining its energy. No, she would have to do things the hard way, for if she was being watched and a series of challenges were coming her way, she needed to be proficient and learn new skills.

The moon rose and the sun set, the winds came, and the rains dragged on. But soon her home began to resemble some kind of liveable dwelling with views all around the bay from her elevated position. It was small and basic though adequate for her needs. The kitchen area was the only serviceable room, with a wooden rocking chair by the hearth and a pallet on the floor. She had put shuttered windows on two opposite sides of her accommodation and erected a split-level door that would allow the light in on sunny days and withstand a battering during the storms.

She smiled, pleased with herself. It had been the most difficult task yet, constructing a home that would keep her safe and dry from the elements.

Now she had to learn to make utilitarian baskets and other serviceable tools if she was to be able to carry food from one place to another.

She raked the ground to make an allotment and began the long laborious job of planting seeds and cultivating herbs. In fact, she spent more hours collecting, processing, and storing her produce than anything else. But it kept her busy, and she wouldn't have time to think about her mother and her sisters or the burden of her loneliness. Nor did she want to worry about her future or what lay ahead.

For now, she just had to get through each day.

CHAPTER FOUR

IT WAS SHADING towards late afternoon when Zolaris called down from the lookout nest. 'Captain, there's land ahead!'

After long weeks away with no land in sight and the ship in tatters after encountering howling gales and turbulent waters, the men needed dry land and the vessel needed an overhaul. The expectant crew peered over the starboard side, seeing nothing more than a smudge of grey uncertainty on the horizon. 'Are you sure?' cried the Captain.

Zolaris eyed through his spyglass again to be sure. 'Yes, it's land, Captain. A small skerry, but definitely land.'

The Captain took out his own battered monocular and gave a reassuring nod. 'It looks barren, but safe enough, I say we dock here and take a look around.'

'We can hunt fresh food again on land,' said Zolaris. 'I am sick of eating fish. My stomach longs for the taste of red meat...'

'And a wench or two to keep you entertained,' came a gravelly voice from the stern. 'That's been a long time as well.'

The crew laughed heartily and exchanged raucous banter as Zolaris scrambled down from his look out post and helped prepare for shore leave. The captain guided the ship towards the mysterious shore where the details of the cliffs and coves soon became apparent and barely-visible reefs held on to the laps of white frothy water.

THE TWO MONTHS it took to reach this island were the most uncomfortable Zolaris had ever spent. Their route took them through unchartered territory and the sky hung cold and grey the entire time. One unchartered sea looked much like the other, and Zolaris knew that, at any time, the curve of the horizon would reveal mysterious shorelines, rugged continents, exotic islands, or another unknown kingdom. These were the best of times and the most profitable of times, for a rich helping of gold and silver would always be hidden somewhere on these lands. Innocents fell like shards of corn under the Captain's sword, and men begged for mercy at the tip of a dirk. Women and children ran for cover, but only a few succeeded. Food supplies were seized and barrels of wine loaded, all the while, the seamen feasted on other men's fear. But their good fortune had run out months ago, and it seemed to Zolaris that he would never be warm again as the chill seeped into his bones.

There were a dozen of them now, yet two months ago there would have been more than two score. Half had been lost to the sea in the storms, the others had died from one of the many ailments that ripped through a stricken ship lost at sea. The faces of the ones who remained were worn and deep lined, their hands rough and swollen, their bodies hunched and carved with scars. These men had travelled many miles and certainly had more than one story each to share.

Two longboats were lowered and made several trips to the skerry, taking the boatmen and supplies for shore leave. The captain picked up a handful of soil as he stepped on to the land. He breathed in deeply as he caressed the contents, then rubbed it between his fingers as he let it tumble back to its resting place. He was tall with a grey pallor about him. His smile was restless, but he tipped his hat when the women approached.

'Good day, Captain,' started Mawi. 'You do not need your swords here. This is a peaceful place. We have no need for such weapons. Please leave them in your boats.'

The men looked at each other with hands on cruel hilts eager for battle, while daggers already stained with blood remained in their boots. The Captain nodded and threw down his sword. The others followed his command. The old crone and two daughters welcomed the visitors with a bounty of fresh fruits and fish, but the men had already decided on their next meal and were keen to venture into the forest.

The Captain yielded a small dirk. 'I will keep this if you don't mind, ma'am. It will be quicker to slit the throat of a boar than wrestle it to death.' He laughed a hearty laugh which echoed round the inlet. Instantly, the island turned grey, a sea breeze stirred, a flock of wood pigeons took flight, and the smell of burnt flesh engulfed the sweetness of the land.

The crone nodded and tilted her head. 'As you wish, Captain, but take care out there, please, and only take what you need.'

The Captain roared with laughter. 'Well, thank you, kind lady. I will certainly take what I need—I think we all will.'

A FEW OF the men soon returned with a wild boar, which they roasted over coals in a pit. A few stragglers appeared a bit later clutching snared rabbits, and another had killed a pheasant. They cracked open bottles of grog and began to enjoy the evening.

Zolaris took every opportunity to flirt with the beautiful Phoebe whose innocence fascinated him in a way that other girls did not. Her features were unlike any girl he had seen before, but he was attracted by more than her extraordinary beauty. This young woman with her long dark hair exuded the charm of a newborn fawn and an exotic princess.

'How would you like to get off this island and come on a journey with me?' he began.

Phoebe didn't respond.

'Surely you want to travel and see the world. There is nothing for you here.' He jutted out his chin as he looked out on the barren landscape.

Still, she remained quiet as she played with the blue ribbon in her hair.

'It's not right that a pretty girl like you should remain

here with no male company and no fun. What's there for you to do? Look after a few scrawny hens and your ancient mother? Best that you leave now while you can.'

She answered him sternly. 'You are wrong. You are so wrong. I have everything I need here. I do not need male company. I have no need to see the world as it is right now. When there is peace, then I will travel. Until such time, this is my home and where I want to remain.'

'There will never be peace,' he retorted as he tore into the meat with crooked teeth. 'Not all the while there are rich pickings to be had.' The meat fat ran down his chin and he laughed out loud as he spread it further with the back of his hand.

Phoebe looked at him now and saw the ugliness of his world. 'In that case, I will remain here forever.'

'Just think what you'd be missing.' He ran a greasy hand up the inside of her leg and tried to reach her milky white thigh.

She pushed it away and shot up out of her chair.'

'Aww, don't be like that,' he said. 'Most girls begin to like it after a while.

'Well, I'm not most girls.' She marched off to sit with her mother.

Zolaris laughed. 'You'll be back. When you realise what a nice little glow you felt just then, you'll come back. They always do.' The lie rolled off the tip of his tongue with ease. They always did.

The air suddenly went cold, the atmosphere heavy. He looked around as the other seafarers dipped their cruel smiles. The old woman levered herself to her feet.

'Gentlemen, gentlemen, let us all get back to enjoying

the evening. I have some very special wine that I keep for special gatherings such as these. Phoebe, can you help me, please.'

Phoebe escorted her mother into the safety of the kitchen. Already a few of the pack were beginning to circle her younger sister. Ellis sat looking straight ahead, not moving, not engaging in conversation. She had witnessed what had happened to her sister. Now she just wanted this awful night to end.

Phoebe looked back at her. She was fuelled with anger.

'I do not feel safe, Mother. There is evil at work here. These men are loathsome and dangerous.'

'I know, daughter. I feel your angst.'

'We need Sansara. She has the power to help us. We are just three women against a dozen men.'

Mawi looked at her daughter. 'Sansara is not ready yet. She still needs time, there is nothing she can do.'

'But, Mother, we must try to summon her. I fear what will happen to us.'

Mawi rested her crooked hands on her daughter's shoulders. 'Phoebe, you have the same powers as Sansara. Please don't forget that. Sansara was chosen to further her skills because her father still lives and she has a message to deliver. You are needed here. Now, believe in yourself and do exactly as I say.'

Phoebe relented and nodded her head in agreement as she followed her mother's instructions. First, they gathered up the prepared vials and added the contents to the goblets and decanters.

'Shall I take the tray out to the men for you, Mother?'

'No, I will finish up here. I want you out of the way now. You have more important matters to attend to, and I have to get a message to Ellis.'

Phoebe nodded.

'Go now, with haste. We have not a minute to spare.'

And within seconds she was gone.

ELLIS STUDIED the table before her, arranged with goblets and decanters filled to the brim. She detected the smell: Hemlock, Aconitum, Laburnum. She didn't dare to look at her mother for she feared her expression would give her away. The crone brushed past her, placing a red handkerchief in her grasp, then she spoke a few words in her ear. Ellis gave a half smile under hooded eyes.

The Captain reached for a decanter and breathed in the aroma. The other men had already averted their attention from Ellis, lured by the liquor and hypnotised by the smell. The pack were laughing and belching, smashing the goblets together, spilling the wine in all directions, and hardly noticing what was going on around them.

Zolaris sniffed at the goblet. He raised an eyebrow and frowned at the smell. He ran a hand through his hair and tilted his head. Ellis quickly averted her gaze. The crone could see everything. He glanced to his right to see three of his shipmates already slumped on the ground. They had barely touched their wine. Another three were dangerously close to the fire in some kind of trance, singing about wood nymphs and sea creatures that were pulling them into the flames. They called for him to join them. His eyes flicked to the crone and then back to Ellis. Where was Phoebe, he thought?

He pushed back his chair and stood tall. *She is waiting for me by the shore. I knew she would.* An expectant smile shivered through his body and he went to investigate. He saw a figure on the boat. He knew it was her. That shape and grace was ingrained on his mind. He submerged himself under the water. *I will surprise her.* It was murky and cold, but his body felt nothing as he glided through the water with ease—towards the boat, towards his reward. The fruits of his endeavours were almost too delicious to comprehend, so he swam faster. He could see the bulk of the ship in the shadows. That excited him. The shiver returned. Carefully, with his dirk between his teeth, he pulled himself up the ladder and crouched low on the deck while he skilfully observed her.

Then a peculiar thing happened. Zolaris felt his blood begin to surge in tribal anticipation. His heart thumped unlike anything he had experienced before. All the slaying he had done, all the blood and yelling, the raping and violating—nothing had ever given him such palpitations. Then there was the most deafening ringing in his ears that caused his eardrums to bleed. He put his palms up to stop the noise. To stop the blood. He couldn't hear. He couldn't move. And then it came at him—a creature so vile and so wound up in anger, with small red eyes and drooling mucus from its gaping mouth, baring wicked incisors and murderous tusks. Zolaris peeled his hands from his ears and tried to aim the dirk. But it was useless. The creature impaled him, and as his feet slipped on the ensuing fountain of blood, the beast rammed the intruder backwards until his head smashed against the stern. The crack from his skull was louder than his screams. The slashing and ripping that followed went on for several minutes. The gurgling croaks only lasted seconds, but the flames of the ship burning lasted most of the night under the gaze of the moon, and then the hull disintegrated to the bottom of the sea into nothing.

When Phoebe returned to the homestead, not one of the pack remained. She looked around. Peace had resumed, and she smiled. All that was evident of the invasion was a pile of grey ashes mixed with the red threads of a handkerchief which Ellis was raking up into a small pile.

'Everything go as planned?' Mawi asked.

'Oh, yes,' said Phoebe wiping a spot of blood from her mouth. 'Most definitely.'

CHAPTER FIVE

THE WINTER PLODDED ON. The snows came and went, and spring returned, as it always does. The new plants were surfacing and that meant extra potions and remedies.

That particular morning, Sansara was woken by a commotion. A fierce roaring and snarling that made her reach for the staff. She stood on the very top of the mound to get a better view and noticed a metallic glimmer racing through the forest—a sheen of silver scales that went on and on, then disappeared again. Then it came to a clearing and she noticed the shape of a creature one only sees in their nightmares. Protuberant eyes flashed yellow and its hinged jaw dropped open, displaying long teeth that could easily rip a hole in the side of her ship. The monster stopped for a moment to sniff the air, and then with a plume of steam blasting from its mouth, emitted a deep guttural roar. The whole forest leaned forward in its ferociousness, the leaves and branches wrenched from their tendons in seconds.

Sansara followed the course of its destination with her eyes, and out in front was a terrified pure white horse. It already had a deep laceration on its flank, and the blood trailed behind it like ribbons of fire. The creature roared again and hurled itself forward with a speed that was quicker than one of her arrows.

Without another moment's hesitation, she shouldered her bow, sheathed the arrows, and picking up the wand, ran towards the place the shadows were chasing. She tripped on an unseen root, falling heavily. She rubbed her shin. *What am I doing?* She realised the danger she was in. Her knees and palms were raw and stinging and blood was running down her leg, but still she pressed on—tearing through the trees and the bare thorn thickets, slipping down the crags and skimming her other shin on the rocks. Through the heather and the gorse she flew and over the brooks she jumped towards a monster that could devour her in one gulp. She followed the roars, but by now, the screams from the horse were louder. *Could she get there in time?* Her beating heart told her 'No!'

The creature could smell her blood. It stopped in its tracks and lifted its huge muzzle into the air. The yellow eyes narrowed and looked straight at her. Sinews of drool hung from the incisors. Its claws were extended and stained red with another victim's blood. She suddenly realised how vulnerable she was and how inexperienced she was. She had only shot down grouse with a bow. An arrow or two would be useless against this brute. She had no other choice here. It roared again and charged towards her. She had no more than ten seconds to align her weapon and fire. With perfect aim, the gnarled wand struck it with venom. The monster snapped in half like a felled tree, its neck severed just below its jaw. With a series of gurgling sounds it slumped to the ground. The wand sank further and the fiend was instantly incinerated. Only a pile of ashes remained, the last piece of evidence of her terrifying encounter. It would soon be dispersed by the wind. With the wand safely returned to her possession, she went to find the stricken horse.

The mare was screaming in confusion and pain. With two open wounds and a gashed leg, it barely had the energy to fight Sansara. As it collapsed on the ground, Sansara thought it was going to die there and then, but she poured the last of the moly onto the open wounds and offered drops of the potion into its mouth. She held out her hand and crooned so softly that her voice calmed the terrified animal. She stroked the young horse and could now see the deep incisions down her chest, probably due to rearing up and fighting back. *'What a warrior you are,'* she whispered out loud and carried on mending the broken animal. With dextrous hands and nurturing fingers, the sorceress found blooms of yarrow and mugwort then gently cleaned the lacerations with iris leaves. The root bulb had to be chewed first to make it pliable and then placed on the laceration. Finally, she covered the unguent with the yarrow. All the time she was humming and chanting and wafting the essence of pressed mugwort to induce sedation. Removing her cape and draping it over the panting animal, the horse began to calm down. Her breathing returned to normal as she gave up fighting the sleep herbs, and the potions began to do their work. The wounded mare slept soundly while the powerful nutrients and minerals were being administered into her body like the flow of oxygen and other essentials being pumped through a life-giving umbilical cord. Slowly, her fibres began the process of repair, and as the hours and days passed, the rate increased. And as the new cells were forged, so she began to get stronger.

Sansara didn't leave the horse's side for several days. She didn't remember sleeping. She certainly didn't eat. She crept under the cloak for warmth when the temperature dropped and checked on the healing process every few hours. It somehow gave her comfort, feeling the strong heart beat against her own and hearing the horse breathing in the still night air. So, she slept with her arm around the horse all night, thinking that perhaps the two of them had found each other for companionship.

Eventually she had to collect more herbs and plants for her own sustenance as well as to make potions and extra moly for her patient. But within a week, her charge was able to get up and walk about, albeit rather slowly.

'I shall call you Pilot. Would you like that name?' She stroked Pilot's muzzle. 'We shall be friends. Well, you are my only friend, actually. I don't know anyone on this island. I didn't even know horses and monsters lived here. But then again, mother always said that monsters and angels live side by side—they just don't realise it.'

CHAPTER SIX

Sansara wiped her hands on her woollen gown and smiled at the horse who was nudging her, trying to work her muzzle into the young woman's hand. It was as if she was pushing her or wanted to take her somewhere. Sansara wasn't really sure.

'I have got to get supplies,' she said to the horse, 'I'm running out of everything now, and I can't venture too far and not be able to find my way back.'

Still, the horse was nudging her, trying to push her, and every step that Sansara took, the horse followed. Pilot was obviously distressed about something. And right now, Sansara didn't quite know what it was.

'Come on, girl. What's wrong?'

Pilot edged forward and waited. Sansara joined her. Then she edged forward again, followed by Sansara.

'Perhaps I should just sit on your back, Pilot. That might be easier.'

The horse nickered and steadied herself, allowing Sansara to straddle her back. She angled her body over the horse's neck and the animal responded with a jolting lurch to speed. The stretch and bunch of Pilot's body was jolting her in a most uncomfortable manner, and she knew that she had to hang on tightly. She crouched down, looked straight between the filly's ears and thundered across the plain. The signals between the young woman and the filly were subtle; it was as if her horse knew what she was thinking before she had even thought it. The animal became an extension of her own body.

The ground was mainly grassland, with fallow fields and low rolling hills, high meadows and stretches of plain between them. It was safe, but she still had to have her wits about her, so as she rode, she sent out her signals and her horse responded. She had never ridden a horse before. Indeed, she had never been on anything that went this fast. But she galloped across the land as if she had been riding forever with the wind in her face and her hair flowing behind her like the waves of a tempestuous sea. She felt the enormous power of the filly beneath her as her strides stretched out to full capacity. She could hear Pilot panting with each motion, and she could see her muscular neck reaching forward and lathering up with the exertion. They lurched across the plains, leaping hedgerows and ditches at this surging pace. The ride was a thrill she could hardly contain. The very idea of going along with a horse in full gallop filled her with a sense of wonder and unrivalled freedom. She had never dreamed such a thing was possible or that the feeling of power would be so intense. The euphoria lifted her spirits to a place way beyond anything else she had experienced before.

They slowed down to a walk and Sansara intuitively took note of their surroundings for spread out before them was a valley that she had glimpsed from her new home. She hadn't fully realised just how lush it really was. Now she could see the long grasses swaying in waves as a gentle breeze blew down from the eastern slope and then leaned into an oasis of colour reflecting the rhythm of the seasons.

As they continued, Pilot stopped by a watering hole surrounded by shady trees and low skimming bushes. There were currants and blueberries stacked on the low ground while sunflowers stood in neat rows next to them, their huge heads full of seeds drooping to the ground. Hazelnut bushes, apple trees, huge soldier pines clinging on to delicious nuts were perched on the higher levels. And the mushrooms and toadstools sat huddled in clusters under a forest canopy along with comfrey, mugwort, snapdragon, and wild pepper.

This was a lavish indulgence provided by the island, and Pilot had brought her here. She felt a lump in her throat as she observed the tranquility and leaned into Pilot to stroke her neck. But Pilot was still moving.

And as they edged in further, she saw a small herd of horses grazing.

There was a young brown colt in the foreground with spindly legs and a wisp for a tail, but he was handsome and strong, pestering his mother for milk. She allowed it as she continued to graze from the succulent grass, her tan body and black mane shimmering as she yanked up tufts of grass.

An impressive black stallion stood by, his head high

in the air, sniffing for intruders, guarding his herd. Other smaller mares and fillies stood by, swishing away nuisance flies, but only the stallion stood guard. Pilot whinnied softly when she saw him. Sansara felt another lump in her throat and dismounted, breathing in the beauty as she followed Pilot towards the leader. Here they touched noses and breathed softly together. He sniffed her muzzle, and as his head bobbed up and down, the other horses came over to extend the greeting.

Now they were all huddled together Sansara could see a beautiful dun mare breathing hard on the ground. She was heavy with foal. In only a few more hours, another life would grace these lands.

But further out from the herd lay a small white body. It didn't move. There were flies all around it. They wouldn't leave it alone. There was clearly something wrong. Sansara was torn. Should she go and see if she could help? Or should she leave it to the herd to sort out? She decided on the former and slowly edged her way to where the body lay. She felt the whole herd watching her as she moved in closer. She was aware of Pilot and the stallion following. Cautiously, carefully, they were letting an unknown into their circle. Neither knew what to do for the best. Her steps were slow. She didn't want to alarm the injured creature, or the rest of the herd.

But when she was right next to it, she fell to the ground and sobbed. She could barely control her emotion as she realised what it was. Pilot came forward and nuzzled it. The stallion stood back to allow the mother to touch her dead baby.

Sansara lightly touched the white fur. A cruel gash

across its neck revealed the tragedy. Had the beast attacked her foal? Did Pilot risk her own life to try and save her infant?

'I'm so sorry,' Sansara said, sniffing back a runny nose. Her eyes were stinging, the breath stuck in her throat. 'If only I had known, I might have been able to get here sooner and save her.'

Pilot nudged the small corpse again. It didn't respond, not even to the gentle sounds of its mother.

'My sweet girl, all I can do is bury your baby. That's all I can do now.' The words fell amongst a myriad of tears. The mother looked stronger than her right now.

'I can't leave your baby here. It will attract predators and the other foals will be at risk. I have to take it away.'

The stallion knew why she had to remove it. So did the mother.

It was the hardest thing she had to do.

In the end, Sansara wrapped the small girl in her cloak and put her across her mother's back. Pilot would stay with her while she convalesced, and her baby would be buried on the mound—overlooking paradise and yet still close to the herd.

CHAPTER SEVEN

That particular winter was the harshest she had ever known. The unforgiving north east winds brought snowdrifts that would punish the island on an unfathomable scale.

The first snow had sifted in silently during the night. Pristine whiteness softened the contours of the familiar landscape, creating a magical dreamland of fantastic shapes and mythical plants. Bushes appeared to grow tall hats of soft snow overnight while the grand old conifers were draped in exquisite glistening soft plump robes. Clouds of billowing condensation hung in plumes where the forest creatures huddled, and frigid icicles clung like jewelled pendants from every available appendage. Sansara had already allowed herself the luxury of fur but didn't waste too much of the magic, just in case her life was in danger again. The cold brought further danger in the form of unwelcome predators. She needed to be vigilant and went out daily to check on tracks and markings left by the foraging animals. The biting air fought hard to chafe her tender young skin, and ice-cold flakes found uncovered patches and froze instantly wherever they landed. She didn't go out unless she had to.

The second snowfall had no magic at all, and the temperature dropped even further. And as the cold took a grip, the squalls grew, and with the squalls and the freeze came the blizzards. By day, the sky was a shimmering blue gauze that sprawled out over the horizon. By night, the sky was full of grey, swollen clouds, and a polished drizzle scattered over the surface of the ground, making all areas impassable and dangerous. Life stood still in these torturous winter months; everything had to conserve its energy until the spring brought the welcomed thaw.

She had stocked up her larder with a regular supply of meat, fish, eggs, berries, nuts and vegetables. The orchard trees had been stripped of their fruit, ready to be made into juices. She had made a shelter for Pilot with lots of bedding close to her own accommodation, and the warmth from the open fire weaved its way out of the closed shutters and into the open barns.

This blizzard lasted for many days and imprisoned Sansara in her dwelling as it unleashed several feet of snow against her door. By the fifth day, the blizzard was howling with an unrelenting full force, and a number of hardy animals had already perished in the forest. They would be welcome food for the predators, she knew. Many trees and bushes would never recover, and the lakes, rivers, and streams would surely flood.

After seven days, the storm had finally blown itself out, and when the wind finally stopped blowing, the last of the snow sifted down. A scraping could be heard outside her hut. She had to push hard to get the door open and found a wolf cub at her door. Pilot was pawing the ground and nodding her head up and down.

'Where on earth have you come from?' said Sansara, looking around for the mother. There were no prints to suggest which direction she had come from, nor was there any blood to suggest an attack. All she could see was a thin little mite that was barely hanging on to life.

Sansara was torn, for she knew if she handled the cub, the mother would surely reject it. But it went against her conscience to abandon it. Maybe an eagle or another large bird of prey had grabbed it and lost it on route and the snow had cushioned its fall. That sort of misadventure was not uncommon. Indeed, it happened many times on her family island where fish would suddenly drop from the sky and you would look up to see a disappointed eagle disappear from view. Some took lambs and fawns, most grabbed rabbits and voles. So a wolf cub landing at her door was not too much of a mystery—especially at this time of the year if this was the runt of the pack and the mother had others to feed.

'You had better come in here, little girl. I will take care of you now.'

She left the top part of her door open and strung up a bag of hay so that Pilot could munch happily and watch the proceedings.

The cub was a fuzzy little creature with a dark brown coat and light blue eyes. She wasn't hurt. Sansara knew that after a careful inspection. Nor did she have a skin ailment. Her eyes and ears looked perfect. Her wispy tail was not broken. She just needed warmth and food, so Sansara carefully lay the pup on a pile of furs while she put some more logs on the fire. She returned to stroke her gently while she got used to her new surroundings. The young animal responded to Sansara's petting by rooting for a place to nurse.

'You're a hungry baby, aren't you?'

The pup continued to root around for her fingers, but that produced nothing. Even with a magic spell, Sansara knew it wouldn't be a good idea. So, she created a mixture of milk from some ground oats and sweetened it with a little honey. She added a drop of yarrow and began to spoon-feed the small animal. She was a hungry girl and polished off the vial quickly. Sansara didn't want to overfeed her, so she ignored the mews and whimpers for more and allowed her to sleep and let the nutrients work.

Every four hours, Sansara fed the baby, and day by day she watched the wolf cub get bigger and stronger. And by the spring, she was running outside in the garden with Pilot. It was almost like Pilot had gotten her baby back, the way she nuzzled her, and let her cuddle up in the barn at night. The young cub would often play with Pilot's long tail hairs—it would keep her amused for hours while Pilot munched on her hay bag or roamed in the meadow. It was certainly good exercise for the cub as she jumped up and down in a vain attempt to grab the swishing tail. Then they would rest a while on the grass while the baby took a nap.

Soon the little one was following her natural instincts and chased the rabbits and deer. She was never successful on these mock hunts. It was all just practise and a deep routed impulse to survive.

Sansara's concoctions kept her going for a long time, and the little rascal even took bits of fish and small birds from her dinner plate—she was such a scavenger. But after a year, she went off into the forest and came back with blood all round her muzzle. She had now learnt to hunt properly.

As a pup, she loved to sit on the mound and practise her howl. It was more of a high-pitched squeak at first, but as she grew larger and more imposing, so did the sonorous call of the wild. One evening, after about two years, a howl was returned. Sansara wouldn't see her again for a long time, she knew that.

CHAPTER EIGHT

As the seasons rolled in and out of yet another year, she began to question her role on the island. She was approaching her fourth spring which marked the fourth year on her own. In that time, she had learnt an incredible amount. She understood that the land, the weather, the seasons, were connected. That the animals, birds, plants and rocks all had lessons to teach and messages to share. That they provided direction, protection, and healing... for survival. She felt such power already from the wealth of the land and had found her journey to be a gratifying one. She had rescued many animals and let them go back into the wild, though they were always sent back with a spell protecting them—they had already endured enough, she thought. She sat with the herd from time to time, checking on the new arrivals and the new mothers. And when an elderly horse began to show signs of age, she would always ease their suffering. She liked to sleep out with the group, if the weather allowed, but when she returned to her mound,

Pilot always trotted back after her, enjoying the mothering.

Her staff had only been used a few times, because mostly she enjoyed the hand to mouth process that she had created: planting seeds, and watching them grow, and then storing the fruits of her labours in the huge jars and vials that she had on her shelves. She had devised ways to make her own clothes and fashioned a loom to weave blankets and rugs. She had made a pile of linen pads to use when she had her monthly bleed and would always rinse them out and feed her menstrual blood into the soil. It was a sort of ritual she had become used to doing with her sisters. But on those days, she felt sluggish so would sit and make more waxen candles and practice different ways to wear her hair. Her favourite was the long braid which coiled like a serpent when she sat down at the hearth.

Her days had become industrious with learning, and she had grown in ways she never thought possible. But just once in a while, a little voice would come into her head and ask 'When will it be time to leave? or Is this my destiny now, to look after myself on the island and all the animals on it?' But the little voice left as quickly as it had surfaced, and she returned to the simple pleasures of restocking her huge assortment of plants and herbs and preparing vials and ointments in case anyone or anything needed it.

With the onset of spring, the flowers had been eager for her touch as she passed by, waiting for nimble fingers to select them and use them for their charms. The trees bowed as she walked through their sanctuaries, with boughs curled to the floor in a salute. She wandered round the island, discovering caves where the bats resided, the forests full of fungi where creatures of the night would dwell, and the sea shore brimming with nutrient-rich kelp and an array of crustaceans and bivalves that made a very satisfying meal. Her garden was a feast of green plants and vibrant blooms, and the allotment brimmed with healing herbs and spices.

ONE DAY, she was collecting molluscs from the shore, and she noticed a sudden change in the weather. A thunderous swell of grey clouds jostled for position, quickly turning a granite sky black, and within seconds, the calm of the day was brewing into a storm. The force of the wind intensified and whipped up tons of dry loose sand from the shore. The rumble of thunder wasn't too far away, and she had to run into the thick of a forest for protection. The rain began to fall softly at first, almost kissing her face with warm gentle drops, but as she hurried into the safety of the glen, the heavens opened and spat out fat bullets that landed on her like lead. She fell under a natural canopy where she sat it out and waited for the bombardment of the storm to pass. A sharp crack made her jump and the following flash of light lit up her claustrophobic surroundings. She heard a tree split and felt the shudder as it fell to the ground. An animal screeched, a grouse took flight—to where she didn't know. On and on the downpour continued. The wind howled through the trees while waves as high as cliff faces surged to within an inch of where she was sheltering.

After a couple of hours, her safe refuge had turned into a morass of devastation where upturned trees had been ripped from the ground and waterlogged trunks and broken branches littered her path. It now looked completely different, and as she tried to find her way out, she found herself trudging amongst a cobweb of trees where every sodden branch, leaf, and sapling slapped her in the face or caught her cloak and tried to hold her back. The storm was still unrelenting and continued to batter the island with a brute force. Tarragon Island was now a maze of muddy narrow tracks and passageways, hindered by corridors of wet bracken, limp foliage, and stinging brambles. Her basket was torn out of her hand by an unforgiving branch. The trees that once bowed to her when she walked past were now gripping their waterlogged roots into the soil. Many could not hang on. The smaller ones were ripped from their sockets like canes and whipped into the air on the swell of a wave and smashed into the tempestuous sea.

She had to get out of the forest. With all the trees upended or on the verge of falling, it was not safe. She pushed on with the wind beating her back, the driving rain forming a shield wall, and all the ghosts from hell slashing against her body as she shuffled forward with tiny steps.

By the time she reached her shelter, she barely recognised it. The door was thrown off its hinges and being tossed in the air by a raging wind. It had already flattened and destroyed her garden—her allotment was a muddy grave. The meadow was under three inches of water. Pilot was nowhere to be seen. Even if she wanted to use the wand, she didn't have the energy to lift it now, let alone launch a command. She feared the wind would take that as well. Instead, she limped into her hovel and sank down on her palette.

By morning she was awoken by the soft nicker of Pilot, standing outside her shelter. The raging storm had burnt itself out, and puffed up white clouds had now come in to hover gently over the island. The sun winked on the dawn, but the devastation was still a morbid reminder.

Still weary and beaten, she rose from her sleep. A shard of light offered a prism for where the door had been. Her voice was jagged as she greeted her friend.

'Were you safe, dear Pilot? I hope the herd is all together.'

The mare bounced her head up and down. Sansara ticked her chin. Pilot lifted her head higher and snorted.

'Are you trying to tell me something again? Is one of the herd in trouble?'

Pilot nuzzled into her and began to push her to the mound. The mound where she watched the sun melt into the sea at night and turned it into a pool of blood red crimson. The mound where she could keep an eye on things and be aware of anything different. This time, her eyes fell on something very different. A coracle next to her own. Thrown here by the storm. no doubt. She had to check who it belonged to. Without delay, she jumped on Pilot's back and headed for the shore.

CHAPTER NINE

She wrinkled her nose against the smell of decaying plants and withered vegetation. Slimy steps and damp cold air tried to impede their path. She felt Pilot skid a few times, going down hard on her rear legs with her front legs out straight to balance. Sansara had to lean forward into her mane and offer reassurance. Moving onto flatter land proved much easier, and Pilot was able to stretch her legs though flying past the devastation at speed revealed the full force of the brutal storm. She would check for animal casualties later, but for now, she needed to check whether a friend or an enemy had migrated to her shores.

The vessel was much smaller than her own coracle, so how it hadn't capsized on the rough sea was a mystery. And though it was still floating, there was a huge amount of water around the single occupant. It was a man—a young man. He was submerged up to his chest. With his arms on the side, he was just about keeping his head above water. He was facing the other way, but his hair hung long and straight past his shoulders. Part of it was held together by a fraying cord, but most of it was a dark tangled mass. A lump on the back of his head bothered her, but the skin was not broken—it was just swollen. She had a remedy for that.

A white shirt clung to his skin, unbuttoned and loose. She could see that he was muscular and strong with a dark skin tone and the hint of hair on his chest. He wore brown breeches that were cropped at the knees, torn in places, but she could fix them easily. She touched his face and he turned towards her. Still unconscious. It was a reflex action that made her jump back. Pilot had found some sea grass to munch on and didn't notice anything behind her.

Sansara leaned in closer to see his face. a more serious wound was just above his right eye, but again, she could fix that. Most importantly, right now, she had to get him out of the boat. He was a dead weight and almost impossible to move. She sat him forwards to grip him under his arms and tried to ease him out that way. His eyelids flickered, and he moaned. She couldn't do it, and she had no idea if he had any internal injuries right now—not until she got him on to the dry land, anyway.

Pilot stepped forward as the man opened his eyes. 'Am I dead?' he asked wearily.

'No, you are very much alive.'

'Where am I?'

'You are on Tarragon Island. My island, and I am going to look after you.'

The man nodded.

'Are you able to stand up?' she asked. 'I have my horse. All you have to do is climb out and she will carry you.'

His eyes opened to navigate the distance. He let out a few deep sighs as he tried to summon some strength.

'I am here and will support your weight. It's not far, I promise.' She continued to coax him.

The man took her arm and pulled himself up. He was tall and lean Even hunched over he was much taller than her. She took his weight on her shoulders as his right arm draped round her. His left arm instinctively gripped his ribs as he stepped out of the boat. She felt him rasp and reassured him. 'It won't be much longer, then I can see to your wounds.'

'I'm so sorry to trouble you like this.' His voice quivered with the strain.

'Don't be silly, I am just glad that you are alive and that I can help.'

'So am I.' He winced as he got out of the boat. Sansara was more nimble and made the stride without too much effort. Pilot edged further into the water and took the man's weight as he fell against her. His arms went over her back and Sansara helped him into a seated position.

'Thank you.' His breath was heavy. 'I am Raoul.'

'My name is Sansara, though we shall chat further a bit later. For now, I want to get you to my home, and I can tend to your injuries.'

Raoul tried to smile, but his wounds were too great. He leaned forward into the mare and let her guide him home.

Sansara led him into her shelter where he sank down onto the palette. First, she soaked a soft piece of fur in an infusion of arnica flowers with yarrow and made a compress for the swelling. She managed to get him to take some willow-bark tea, holding him up as he sipped the soothing liquid. Laying him back down, she carefully cleansed the dried salt from his face, checking for cuts and scratches as she worked. He reached up for her hand.

'Thank you, Goddess.'

She smiled and stroked his face. 'You must rest now. Let me fix you. I can make you better.'

He smiled briefly in return and then succumbed to the aromas wafting around him, and gradually, and as if by magic, a handsome face emerged.

She boiled a comfrey root and mashed it to a pliable pulp. That mixture would bind the skin together above his right eye. But first she had to flush the wound out with clean water, making sure that no fragments or splinters had got trapped inside it. Adding some marigold petals to the mixture, she placed the warm unguent to do its job.

She removed his wet shirt and cleaned his body with a fresh piece of rabbit fur. He was bruised all over his torso, and his skin had turned purple and black in places, but the arnica infusion would reduce the discolouration. Thankfully, he had no broken bones, but the bruising would make him immobile for several days.

She had to remove his trousers. She had never seen a naked man in her entire life. In fact, she had never been this close to a man except when the seafarers invaded Mawi's Island. Even then, they were a safe distance away, and she didn't even detect what they smelt like. This was a completely different experience altogether.

Coming back to the present, she had to snap out of her dilemma. He would get a chill if she left him much longer in those wet clothes. So quickly and without too much effort, she managed to cut the ripped trousers away. Once he was cleaned and dried, she checked for broken bones and was relieved when he displayed just one gash and a few scratches and bruises. Placing the comfrey unguent on his skin and making the marigold into a paste, she sealed the injury with some iris leaves and spread the rest of the arnica potion over his bruised legs. Draping him with a soft blanket, she heard him murmur under the covers and knew that he was more comfortable. Only then did she sit back, hugging her knees to her chest and leaning against the wall. She needed to see him breathe, to watch the downy blanket softly rise and fall with each intake of air. She didn't move for several hours. She just watched him sleep and waited for the healing nectar to work. But his sleep was full of demons and he thrashed at them constantly. She wiped his brow with ice cool water and chanted soothing words. But he didn't feel anything —he couldn't hear her words of comfort.

Inside his head, the nightmare wouldn't let go. His world was full of black and cold. It was also wet and putrid. The darkness pitched his eyes. The storm had lasted for hours. The sun had forsaken him. His arms burned where he had been holding on so tightly. His hands were red raw with the strain. There was so much water in his craft that swelled further with each penetrating wave. The cold had become a numb presence that was slowly devouring him, the wet sea water seeped into his bones and he felt the shiver again. He was curled up—rocking, hiding, keeping his eyes firmly shut so that the hungry creatures couldn't see him. A pair of hunting eagles didn't even notice him hunched and lifeless in his reluctant womb. They were too high up. The clouds were too low and ferocious: full of anger, full of rain, piercing his skin like daggers. Unrelenting, unforgiving. The ice-cold water lapped around him like a hundred forked tongues. He couldn't move. It was too painful. He tried to straighten his back. The bump on his head was throbbing. His head was pounding, and he felt the vomit rise in his throat. He knew he would throw up soon. The vessel rocked and swayed, throwing him around, but still he hung on. He groaned several times and rolled around in his cocoon. He thought he was going to die. If he wasn't already dead, he knew it wouldn't be long now. It went dark again as he gave in to exhaustion.

The storm had long abated when a mist began to cover him in the death veil. He felt for blood. There was none. He pressed his fingers around his torso to detect a wound. He winced with the pain. That meant he was still alive. He looked up into sky. The eagles continued to swoop and soar on seraph wings, the majesty of their power commanded awe. The sun caught the tip of a feather and turned it golden. He turned his head to see the mist devour it instantly. That meant they couldn't see him. But he would be flying with them soon. He knew it wouldn't be long. His cocoon bobbed and rocked from side to side, moving with the waves. rolling with the tide. Nauseating.

And then it stopped. He was too tired to look or was he too scared, he didn't know which. Neither did he have the energy to lift his head. It still smelt of rain, the air was still damp. He still felt pain. Where was he?

But then he felt a different sensation. He felt safe again. He felt warm. He heard a female voice talking to him. She was helping him. His dreams became less urgent. His head didn't hurt anymore. His ribs didn't ache. And as the pain began to subside. So did the fear. He could relax now. He let himself drift off to a better place when he felt someone watching over him. He was somewhere full of love. He could close his eyes without the nightmares now. He wasn't going to die. He knew he had been saved. A breath of fresh air filled his lungs, and a beam of light made him smile. His blood flowed warmer round his body and the sleep came easy.

CHAPTER TEN

A BREEZE BROUGHT the waft of stagnant water and rotting vegetation through a gap in the door. She looked over to Raoul and saw that he was settled at last. Pulling the rug over his shoulders, she went to the door to view the devastation. Everywhere she looked was limp and shrunken, submerged and drowning. For as far as the eye could see, no colour remained, only browns and greys, and a heavy mist had wrapped itself around the island as if to banish the sun forever. It would take years to recover. Some areas would never heal—that was plain to see.

A familiar figure arrived at her door in the form of the she-wolf. Sansara was pleased to see that she had fared well. She extended her hand so the wolf could smell her and then she got a tickle under the chin. Behind, her cubs followed, and hovering in the bushes was the alpha male: huge, dominant, powerful.

Sansara got down to her level and stroked the she-wolf affectionately. 'How have you been, my beauty? I have missed you so much. I think Pilot has missed you, too.'

Pilot came over to nuzzle the wolf. The affection was returned ecstatically with a series of jumps and yelps. Her tail spun around, almost knocking her little ones over who ran about excitedly between her legs.

'And look at your family. How proud you must be.'

She saw the male edge closer.

'I expect you are hungry, aren't you, with a growing family to feed.'

The she-wolf playfully tugged at her arm as if in a mock fight. Sansara knew it was a sign of affection and not aggression. Still the male hung back... keeping alert in case he needed to lunge.

'I'll get you some food, my friend. I know it must be hard for you right now. But just you watch the spectacle. Your mate might just come up and nuzzle my arm as well.'

She reached round for her staff and as she thrust it into the air, a translucent cloud burst from its shaft. The glare shocked the alpha male to retreat for a moment, but keeping an eye on his family, he moved forward again. The cubs hid under their mother, whimpering and jostling. The she-wolf stood firm. The cloud grew strong and fierce and sucked up the debris like a spiralling tornado, scouring the land for sludge and mud. Within moments, gallons of water had been extracted from the deluged soil. Once the cloud was full, Sansara sent out another blast and it vanished from sight... to empty its deluge in some other vortex, she demanded. Then she curved the staff into an arch and created a rainbow of light which brought a palette of colour to the island again.

Minute by minute, the contours bloomed, trees climbed higher, and the scent of life breezed through the windows. The sky returned to its natural shade of azure, and the lake responded. A brand new carpet rolled out on the hills to reveal vibrant blooms and joyful colours. The hares jumped, the lambs frolicked, and the horses bucked. Life had returned to the island.

With another tap on the ground, she provided food for the wolves. It was then that the alpha male ran up to her, and with his front paws on her shoulders, reached down to lick her face.

'I know you are pleased, my beautiful boy, and I hope we can be friends now.' He continued to lick her face in joyful emotion and jumped down when Sansara ordered a juicy red steak especially for him.

She stood for a moment or two, watching the lay of the land change back to what it was before. And her heart strings pulled at the sight of the cubs having their first meal in a very long time. She laughed out loud at the sound of them pushing and jostling, but the mother and father were too busy themselves to sort them out.

'Don't worry, Pilot. I'm not going to leave you out.' She conjured up a bucket of oats and a bag of hay. Pilot nickered in response and submerged her head into the bucket.

'Well, that's the first time I've ever seen anything like that.'

Sansara spun around at the sound and looked at Raoul, propped up on one elbow, watching her.

CHAPTER ELEVEN

It was morning. The sun hovered just above the trees casting earth's first shadows. Her face bore a look of happiness, eyes bright and wide, lips just parting, long dark hair spiralled in a coil that hung to her waist. But he had watched her. He had seen everything.

Sansara stared back at him. She couldn't help herself, though she knew it would make him feel awkward. He had discovered her secret, and there was nothing she could do. She would have to tell him the truth. But that wasn't the reason that made her stare. It was because he was so handsome. Of course, she had spent several hours looking at him while he was asleep—she hadn't left his side. But that was when he lay with his hair brushed off face, covered with a poultice on his eye, and an unguent on his body. And yes, the symmetrical features and strong jaw had been plain to see. But now, with straight black hair falling past his chin and vivid blue eyes set in a thicket of black lashes, he was like a magnet. He must have put a spell on her when she wasn't looking, she thought. For long seconds, she stared, held there suspended, and she couldn't seem to look away. And he stared right back at her with the curl of a smile lingering in the corner of his mouth. She tore her eyes away from him as the flush rose up to her cheeks and looked to the ground as she tried to regain her composure.

She was probably the most beautiful woman he had ever seen. Certainly the strongest. No wonder she was able to pull him up out of the boat and support his weight. *Did she use that wand to save him?* Was the horse magic as well? And the wolves? A woman who commanded respect from an alpha male—now that was even more incredible than turning a dying island into a paradise again.

When the beam of rainbow light burst through the shutters, he thought he was dreaming. But when he sat up and removed the poultice, he saw what she was doing through the open door. He was relieved when she turned around, for it proved he wasn't hallucinating.

There was an innocence about her, as if she had never seen a man before, and yet her body was that of a mature woman. Though he instantly felt as if she bewitched him—such was the effect she had on him, even if she wasn't a sorceress—he would still have found her enchanting.

'I'm sorry. I didn't mean to embarrass you.' His voice was like velvet to her ears.

'No, no, you didn't embarrass me, I am just surprised to see you up so soon.'

He rubbed the back of his head and winced. 'Well, I might have still been asleep if I hadn't been woken by spells and magic.' He dipped his chin while still looking at her and was pleased to see her furtive expression crack into a warm smile.

'I haven't ever done that before.' Her face flushed again. 'Well, not to that extent.'

'It was very impressive, and the wolves enjoyed it the most, I do believe.' His chin jutted out to the family grooming themselves in the sun.

'Yes, poor things. Now there will be food for all the animals again.' She looked at them adoringly but turned back quickly when she heard him moan.

'Here, let me help you sit up. You can have this rocking chair by the fire.'

'Where will you sit?'

'I have another wooden chair here at my table, I will move it round.'

She poured him a cup of willow-bark tea and cut off a hunk of bread. 'I will make something a bit more substantial when I have been out in the garden.'

He looked at her quizzically again.

'I don't do everything with magic you know—only when I have to.'

He smiled as he eased himself back into wearing the clean shirt and newly sewn breeches. 'Thank you for saving me and cleaning me up.'

'You are very welcome.' She sat down opposite him and sipped on her tea. 'So, tell me how you got washed up on my island. I haven't seen another soul for many years, you know.'

'Well, your story sounds far more interesting than mine. But I will tell you my story, if you will tell me yours after.'

She nodded. 'That's a deal.'

CHAPTER TWELVE

'I REMEMBER the excitement surrounding my first sea voyage,' he began. 'Leaving my comfortable homestead behind, my mother tearfully waving me off with her handkerchief, and my father comforting her with a strong arm around her shoulders, though they knew it was the start of an adventure for a twenty-year-old lad. It was something I had wanted to do from when I was a small boy: to be an ardent explorer. My grandfather used to tell me stories about seafarers finding hidden continents or small island gems. Of shipwrecks and monsters, and pirates and buried treasure. Though, for me, it was more about the being the first to discover something, to be one of the first to walk on unchartered territory and leave my mark somewhere. So, with a heavy heart, my parents let me go, and even helped me secure a position on a boat.

'It was a grey morning when I wandered down to the harbour to board my waiting ship. The chill was biting and whipped across my face without reason. This same raw chill was to follow me from that very day.'

He took another sip of willowbank and pulled his rug up to his cheeks.

'The ship was very similar to yours, I remember: a lean vessel with a high prow. It bore the figurehead of a serpent; but it was the wealth of savage-looking sailors that unsettled me more. Half of them had black teeth while many of them had no more than one or two that hung jagged from discoloured gums. Their beards did little to conceal the monstrosity, and their rags and old furs merely added to their animal-like persona.'

Sansara winced at such a spectacle.

'I remember how the narrow plank heaved and swayed dangerously, and I had to hang on for dear life. I lost my hat to the wind which caused an eruption of laughter from the deck as I tried to catch it. Hanging on to my bindle, and on to the rope, as well, caused much amusement among the ranks. All these toothless grins laughing at me as if I were merely put there for their entertainment. But I laughed along with the best of them, even though I didn't find it amusing at all.'

Sansara put a hand up to hide her broadening smile.

The look didn't go unnoticed by Raoul. 'I went below deck to secure a bed and lay out my few belongings, then I ventured back up to get my orders and prepared to sail.'

"Ever been on a ship before, lad?" A burly sailor asked me.

"Oh yes, many times." I lied. The sailor flipped his chin up as if to say If that's your story lad, then who am I to disbelieve you. But, of course, he didn't believe me. I looked no more a sailor then than I do now, but I

was eager to sail around the world and explore the wondrous things that no one else had seen. I yearned to be an explorer.'

Sansara nodded in agreement. She had to venture to new continents to find her calling and was yet to discover more. She stopped in mid thought as Raoul carried on.

'THE CAPTAIN, a leathery man of undeterminable age, took his place at the tiller, and the oarsmen took up their places. I was sent up to the crow's nest by the burly sailor, and the ship surged ahead, making for the open sea.

'Weren't you scared up in the crow's nest?' she asked with concern.

'Yes, I was terrified, but I wasn't going to let anyone know that. I shimmied up there as if I had been doing it all of my life.'

Sansara laughed, to which Raoul grunted in return. He winced as he held on to the ache at his side. Sansara rose quickly in concern, but Raoul gestured for her to remain sitting. He still had a long way to go.

'I slept that night in unbelievably cramped quarters. One minute, I thought I had loads of room, with a spacious hammock and a bearable odour. But by the time it came to bedding down for the night, it seemed that all the oarsmen had decided to kip down with me, and I had to sleep with a blanket over my head. The smell was quite awful.'

Sansara wrinkled her nose at the thought.

'After a couple of weeks, we were making progress

with a good prevailing wind. The sails were raised, and most of the men were able to rest. I stood on the deck, looking out to sea and suddenly I spotted something. I nudged the chap next to me and pointed to what I had seen. He shimmied up the crow's nest and shouted down to us.

"Land ahoy?"
"Is it an island?" I called up to him.
"No, it looks like stone or slab coming out of the water..... wait a minute.... there's lots of them ... and they look like towers."
The Captain stood on the bow and took out his spyglass. "He's right, you know. It looks like a buried city"

Raoul noticed Sansara's fixed gaze and paused briefly to finish his tea. He nodded when she gestured to pour him another cup. She took her stance again when she had refilled both cups, and, leaning forward with her chin on the heel of her hand, she pressed him with raised eyebrows to know what happened next.

'The news of an underwater city travelled fast, and half-dressed men clambered up from below, all eager to witness this forgotten ruin. Some men were arguing that it was just a mass of rocks, but the closer we moved towards it, the more apparent it became.'

Sansara had her eyes wide open now.

'The captain had never seen anything like it. He said that in all his twenty years as a seafarer, he had little to show for his explorations, and this was too exciting an opportunity to miss, so he prepared to drop anchor.'

'I have never seen a ruined city, either,' exclaimed Sansara. 'I should love to, though.'

Raoul raised one eyebrow at her retort. He responded with a low *'hmmm,'* and carried on.

'Then suddenly, alongside the ship, came the most beautiful sea creatures you have ever seen. Certainly, I had never seen anything like them. They were smooth and silver, almost a blue-grey colour, but their smiling faces were their most amazing characteristic. They performed tricks in the water and jumped alongside us. They were like acrobats and clowns with their dazzling skills. Everyone was cheering and laughing.'

Sansara looked at him in earnest, her lips parted in anticipation.

'These mammals swam round the ruins, curling around each other, then they all dived to the depths. As we looked down, what looked like the remains of a palace appeared. The towers were ornate and spiralled down for several fathoms. The bricks were grey and mottled, the texture was of slate. One man shouted that he could see treasure, and another called out that he could see gold. Most of the men swore they could see mermaids—and one by one they started to jump in. Someone threw me overboard. *"Get in there and find yourself a mermaid. Might make a man out of you yet"* he yelled out. I could still hear him laughing as he jumped in after me.

'I had got caught in a coracle on the side of the ship. I couldn't free myself. I was clinging onto the ropes and shouting for help. I could feel my shirt ripping from the seams. It bunched up and held me there suspended. I didn't know what was keeping me there, but I hung on to the ropes regardless.

'The beautiful gliding creatures had swum away by now, probably from all the noise we were making. With all the men splashing in the water, shouting and laughing and climbing on the turrets, it was quite an alarming spectacle. But, suddenly, there was this huge roar, and the spikes that rose from the sea like towers rose from the depths like teeth. The treasure that the sailors thought they had seen were scales, and *the mermaids* were the deep yellow eyes of a monster. It rose out of the sea like a serpent, its forked tongue flailed back and forth like a whip from its unhinged jaw. And when its body breeched the waves, I saw a thousand scales shining like wet tar as the sea water clung to them. We had awoken a sleeping giant.

'The ship was rocked from side to side as it thrashed about. Tidal waves slammed into the hull. I managed to heave myself into the small coracle and slide down so I would not be seen. I could hear screaming men and gurgling cries for help. The ocean spray was crimson now, and the roar of the awoken beast was unlike anything I had heard before. I saw the huge tail as it came down to thrash the ship in half. My coracle was dislodged at once, and I was propelled far from the squall. I could still hear the sounds of death, of drowning men and bodies being ripped in half. But there was nothing I could do. Nothing at all. I had no oar or paddle, and even if I had managed to use my hands to get within a foot of the men, the creature would have torn me to shreds as well.

'The strength of its wrath propelled me far from the disaster, and as the serpent lowered itself to its slumber again, nothing of the ship remained. I was the only survivor.' He stopped and took in a few breaths as he relived the encounter.

'Oh, my goodness, Raoul. And you think that my story could surpass that? I don't think so.'

He shrugged his shoulders in response and pushed out a deep breath through his nose. 'I was lucky, Sansara. Really lucky. I had the Fates with me that day. But I remained in the coracle for days... long days which morphed into one long nightmare. I didn't know whether it was night or day most of the time. I slept for long periods. I tried to catch fish—unsuccessfully. And then came the self-doubt. I should have gone back for them. I could have saved one, maybe two. I thought I was going mad. I thought my Fates had forgotten me. But then the storm came... and brought me to you.'

Sansara levered herself out of her chair and leaned forward. She stroked the hair from his brow and then touched the side of his face with her cupped hand. He reached up to take it in his own and kissed it before holding it to his cheek.

'You did nothing wrong, Raoul. Those coracles are only meant for a couple of people. If you had made it back to them, then they would all have tried to get in. But you have already said you had no paddle. It would have been impossible to reach them. Yes, it is a tragedy that those poor men died, but you are not to blame. They made the decision to jump in when they hadn't determined the dangers. Please erase that thought from your mind.'

'You are right, dear Sansara. Of course, you are right. But this is my destiny. This is my journey of hope. The Fates did not desert me as I imagined so many times out there. The winds brought me to your shores. Not only was I saved from the mouth of a sea serpent, I was also brought to you.'

She leaned into him tenderly again and kissed his cheek. 'You must be hungry now. I will fix us some dinner, and after we have eaten, I will share my story with you.'

'Now, this I am longing to hear.'

He leaned back with his eyes closed and stretched his toes out to the fire. He could hear the sounds of Sansara preparing their food beside him and humming a delightful tune. But he didn't see her wafting a spell over him so that he would forget what he had seen her do. All he would remember was how a beautiful woman had saved his life and how she told him her story of how she was born and raised on the island, and that she lived alone there now.

'I HAVE BEEN SPARED *by an angry sea serpent and saved by the beautiful Sansara. What a fine story we can tell our grandchildren when we are old and grey.*'

CHAPTER THIRTEEN

A BREEZE CURLED around his face, bringing an image of long hair blowing around him and carrying the scent of food to his nostrils. He opened his eyes. Sansara was already up and preparing breakfast.

'How are you feeling today?' she asked him, aware of his movement.

'Much better, thank you.' He sat up and felt the back of his head, pleased that the swelling had gone down.

'And your eye injury? I see that has healed quickly as well.'

'Yes,' he replied, lightly touching the newly formed scab. 'You certainly have magic hands.'

She smiled back at him. 'It's the herbs and plants that I use. They are the magic, not I.' She turned back to carry on with her dough making.

'I love the taste of fresh bread,' he said, remembering how his mother used to bake loaves and rolls for the family.

'So do I. It's my favourite thing to bake. Mother used to make it for us often.'

He remembered how she had told him that her mother had to go away for a while, and so now Sansara was fending for herself on the island. He didn't press for any further clarification.'

'Shall I go and collect some eggs for you?' he offered.

'Already done,' she replied.

'Well, let me go and get some more firewood, then. I need to do something in return for your kindness.'

'That would be most helpful, Raoul, thank you.' She nodded to him and turned away as he pushed himself off the palette.

Sansara had left a clean basin of water beside the bed, so he washed his face and hands, donned a fresh set of breeches that Sansara had left out for him, shrugged into a newly woven shirt, laced up a brown leather jerkin, and pulled on a pair of brand new boots.

'How do I look?' he asked.

She turned to see him standing upright, his long dark hair was combed into place, and dark blue eyes stared out at her from a suntanned face. She had to curtail the blush for fear of giving her inner most thoughts away—for she found him to be most handsome with a strong body and a kindly demeanour. She wiped her hands on her apron and went to move an invisible thread from his shoulder. He took her hand in his and planted a kiss on it.

'Thank you for everything. I would certainly have died without your help.'

'You are most welcome, Raoul.' She held his gaze and

smoothed down the material covering his arms. 'But don't be long now. Breakfast is nearly ready.

'I won't. I promise. I'll be as long as it takes to work up an appetite.'

OUTSIDE, he put his hand to his brow to shade him from the early morning sun, and his gaze took him to the shimmer of the lake where a thousand crystal stars were still dancing from the night before. *I shall take a dip in there later today*, he thought to himself. *That is the most inviting water I have ever seen.* He continued to scan the horizon and settled on the vast mountain range tinged pink and gold from the rising sun.

Raoul continued to stare out across the glittering azure sea. And as his eyes brought him back to the island, he saw a land covered in beautiful colours that clung to the surface in clumps. A gentle breeze cooled the very edges, and he could hardly believe how nature could change so dramatically from a vision of peace and contentment to the raging pits of hell. But then again, in his relatively short time on this earth, he had come to know the changing manner of some, for that's exactly how men behaved. Nature was merely a mirror of man's existence.

He grabbed the axe leaning against the chopping stump and ventured into the forest to cut up more firewood. He found lots of fallen oak branches and a couple of hickory trees—these made fine logs for burning, as they burnt cleaner and longer. He collected a sturdy pile and then began the process of splitting them for the hearth.

His action was clean and precise, raising the axe high above his head and raining it down hard so the blade split each piece right in the centre. *How had Sansara done this on her own?* he thought. Shaking his head in disbelief, he carried on in awe, only stopping to wipe his brow or take a swig of water from the flagon. Once he had split a substantial load, he washed his hands in the outside pail and went inside to find Sansara laying the table.

'Just in time,' she observed, handing him a plate of eggs and wild mushrooms with a large wedge of freshly cooked bread.

'This is divine.' His eyes lit up at the plate in front of him. 'And afterwards, I was thinking of going for a swim in the lake. Would you care to join me?'

Sansara sat down opposite him, tore off a corner of bread and dipped it into her runny egg. 'Well, I will certainly come down to the lake with you, and I would love to stand in it. But I won't be able to swim with you.'

'And why is that?' He looked up at her with a furrowed brow.

She swallowed hard before she could reply. 'Because I cannot swim.'

Raoul looked at her, his expression incredulous. 'You cannot swim?'

She carried on eating and shook her head. 'No, I have never learnt.'

He was dumbstruck. This woman who could do everything, it seemed—one who could fell and chop wood, who could make a fire and build a home, who could survive on an island with only a horse for company —she couldn't swim.

He shook his head. 'Well, I shall teach you then.' He swallowed another morsel of bread soaked in the runny yellow egg.

She looked up at him. 'Really?'

'Yes really. This very day.'

They carried on with their breakfast, both smiling at the thought of it, and it was just one more thing that he could help her with.

CHAPTER FOURTEEN

The lake was a majestic piece of the landscape with azure and jade ribbon shimmering in the late afternoon sun. Reeds grew thick in the shallows along the banks, and Sansara smiled when she saw a water vole skimming across the surface, spreading ripples as it moved. The mountains loomed ahead of her like a crowning glacier of white. And stretching out behind her were the great grasslands with their bountiful source of life. Young flowers began to unravel in their camouflaged cocoons while others were already in full bloom. The waves of softly billowing grasses turned the meadows into a beating heart.

Raoul watched her disrobe from his vantage point and smiled with a growing affection. He thought her to be the most exquisite woman he had ever seen with her beautifully sculpted body and finely chiselled features. How could such a beauty have remained so isolated on this idyllic but remote island? Though lucky for him she had, he thought. He watched her dip her feet tentatively in the shallows. He could tell that the water was freezing cold when she recoiled quickly with the shock and held her hands up to her exposed breasts.

She looked at her naked body in the reflection. Already she felt that she had changed so much—not just mentally, but physically as well. She ran the palm of her hand over her neck and over her muscular, well developed shoulders. Her arms were toned and strong. She felt the fulness of her breasts and the corrugation of her ribs protecting a flat abdomen of superior strength. Her hips were nicely rounded with the curves of womanhood, and her legs were well defined. She bowed down to the water and the reflection smiled back at her. She saw the shape of adulthood—her eyes looked larger and her lips were fuller. It was a face of learning, of strength, of courage. For the image did not just reflect her appearance. It reflected her determination and perseverance.

Slowly and carefully, she eased herself in until she was completely submerged. The warm sun beamed down on her skin and she quickly adjusted to the temperature. She closed her eyes and looked up to the orb, feeling the rays warming her face and neck. Breathing in deeply, she embraced the afternoon. Days like these made her feel alive and reborn. Her skin tingled like she had shed a complete layer, and she felt refreshed again. She swirled the water around her legs with the tips of her fingers and wriggled her toes in the folds of silt. Her hands scooped up a palm of water, and she splashed it over her face. Tiny fish swam up to her and she giggled at their touch. They nibbled her toes and the feeling was actually quite therapeutic, she thought.

She turned to see Raoul wade into the lake, making his own swirling patterns as he pushed through the water. She gasped when she saw his body glistening wet in the sunlight, the beads of water rolling off his skin like pearls.

He launched in and dived down quickly, then resurfaced right beside her and flicked his head to the side to get the hair out of his eyes. 'Bbrrr this is cold.' He chattered, his teeth clenched together and his mouth turning a light shade of blue.

'It certainly is,' she replied, swishing the water with her hands.

'I think we had better keep moving, then we will warm up.'

'I think so, too,' she replied. She could feel herself beginning to cool down, so she moved more vigorously.

'If you watch me first, I will show you how to swim.'

'Okay, I will keep watching you.'

She didn't take her eyes off him as he dived into the water again. After coming up for air, he reached out with his arms then pulled them round to his sides. His legs were kicking the way a frog would move itself along, and he glided through the water with ease. Turning around, he dived down and as he breached the water, he was next to her again.

'Your turn, now,' he said, invigorated with the swim and feeling warm again.

'Will you hold me?'

'Of course, I will hold you, Sansara. You will be safe with me. I promise.'

The trust prompted her to stretch right out. Her arms

were in front of her, and the inner sides of her hands were touching while her legs were straight behind her.

His hands supported her waist. 'Now keeping your head up, I want you to move your arms in wide circles. That will keep you afloat. I will be holding you, but don't stop moving your arms.'

'Like this?' She did her wide circles in the water exactly as he had taught her.

'That's great, Sansara, that's absolutely perfect. Now I want you to pretend you are a frog. Keeping your arm circles going, I want you to kick back like a frog.'

'Okay, but you will still hold me?'

'I won't let you go.'

Propelling herself along with a frog-leg kick-back, and keeping afloat with her circling arms, she began to move forward... and moving quite fast. Her arms were strong from all the lifting and chopping, and her legs were muscular from walking and riding. Therefore, this energetic movement came quite naturally to her. After a while, when Raoul swam up beside her, she realised that she had been swimming on her own.

'I knew you would be a natural. You are incredible.'

'But so are you, Raoul. You taught me.'

He put his arm round her waist and drew her in closer. She felt a tug between them, as if they were tethered together, the rope pulling tighter and tighter with each breath. His eyes didn't leave hers, and she felt his caress, drawing her into her very soul with some mysterious force.

The Fates have sent him, she thought. The Fates have given her a companion. They have seen the good that she has done, the years spent on her own, and they have rewarded her. She gazed at him, her lower lip caught between her teeth, for a long, considering moment. Then, brushing the hair from his face and cupping his cheeks in her hands, she looked into his piercing blue eyes and planted a kiss on his lips.

He looked back at her extraordinary beauty, her magnificence, her determination to succeed, and holding her even tighter, he thought, *I will never let you go. Not now, not tomorrow, not ever.*

CHAPTER FIFTEEN

Capricious clouds had been tantalising the sun all morning but had eventually given way to a clear day. It was summer, and Raoul's injuries had completely healed. He had spent the past four months fishing, fixing fences, helping her on the allotment with weeding, raking and planting, and of course, chopping wood ready for the winter. In those few months. their friendship had grown into something quite special. She noticed how he looked at her with adoration. She had never seen anyone look at her the way he did, certainly not a man. His eyes sparkled with respect and admiration when she spoke. His voice was always full of praise when she did something. He always put her first in everything they did. Sometimes she found herself blushing at his humbling words and found it hard to accept such praise. He was the perfect companion, and always listened to her intently when she wanted to talk.

Something else was also changing as their relationship grew. An accidental touch made her warm inside, and when he stood behind her to give her a hug, she glowed. And as they teased and joked and laughed together, the subtlest, most innocent of gestures took on a completely different meaning. Shen out walking by the shores, they would always find an abandoned cave. Here, they would light a fire and make tea, or cook a squirrel or a grouse for supper, and lay in each other's arms till the chill of the morning awoke them again and they would return refreshed to the homestead.

This particular morning, Sansara was braiding her hair at the table and Raoul was cleaning his boots on the outside stool.

'I think we should go riding today.'

Raoul pushed a cautious laugh through his nostrils as he admired the clean leather. 'Me, ride a horse?'

'Yes, both of us together. It will be such fun.'

'And where are we going to get two horses?'

'Come with me and I'll show you.'

She had already packed a bag of food and drink for their venture and had slipped into a pair of linen breeches and a light cotton shirt. He was already attired in working clothes. Taking his hand, she led him down the pathway to the herd. The vista was painted golden, green, and purple, and the majestic backdrop of the mountains was still lined with a thin covering of snow. An aura of yellow tinged the landscape and the welcome sounds of the year's second half filtered through the air. As they approached the lake, its morning mist had lifted, and the sun was playfully bouncing off the surface.

The herd was in their usual place, the stallion still in his periphery position. He had not been challenged this year. But Sansara knew there wasn't another male who could match him for that prized position. She did notice a few new foals had been born, though, swelling the herd to an impressive count of thirty.

Pilot came up immediately and nuzzled her soft nose into Sansara's cheek.

'I think she likes you,' observed Raoul.

'We go back a long way,' said Sansara. 'I rescued this one as well.' She kissed her muzzle and stoked her warm cheek.

'So, we have something in common then.' Raoul smiled and patted Pilot on the neck.

The black stallion had become aware of an intruder and was making his way over. His head was bouncing up and down, his tail brushing away nuisance files.

'Do I need to be worried?' said Raoul, stepping back from the mare.

'No, not at all. He just wants to make sure you are not a threat. Here, give him some of these oats.'

Raoul held out his hand flat and the stallion, softly and delicately, removed every oat without dropping one morsel on the ground.

Raoul was quite impressed and began to acquaint himself with the stallion.

'Hello there, handsome boy, and what has Sansara called you?'

Raoul looked at Sansara while the stallion searched for more food.

'I haven't named him yet. I only gave Pilot her name because she spends so much time with me.'

'So, this one is a bit elusive, then?' The horse had sniffed out Raoul's apple, and the new admirer had to give in. 'I've got a good name for him.'

Sansara looked at him with a withering look. 'It has to be a good one. It has to suit him.'

'Of course. I think he should be called Porter, because he looks after all the horses on Tarragon Island.'

Sansara smiled and nodded her head, her lips puckered into a thoughtful curve as she mulled it over. 'Pilot and Porter. Yes, I like that. He now has a name at last.'

Raoul was stroking him and, at the same time, being nudged backwards while Porter searched for more food.

'Porter will be the horse you are going to ride today.'

'What? A stallion?'

'Yes, a stallion. He will be fine. I promise you.'

Sansara stepped forward and whispered something in Porter's ear.

'What did you say to him?' said Raoul, his voice low, his eyebrows meeting in the middle.

'I told him to be gentle with you, otherwise, there would be no more apples.'

Raoul laughed nervously. 'It's that simple, eh?'

Sansara nodded in return. 'Yes, it is.'

Porter stretched out his front legs and lowered his hind quarters to let Raoul climb on his back. The young man looked back at Sansara. 'Are you sure about this?'

'Yes, I'm sure. Porter will be fine.'

Raoul gripped onto the coarse black mane and heaved

himself into the seated position. He stroked Porter's neck and telling him there would be no more apples if he got bucked off. Sansara laughed at the two of them becoming more acquainted. She hoisted herself into position and led Raoul into a slow walk while he adjusted to the movement.

'Are you okay?'

'Yes, I really like this. Me and Porter are going to get along just fine.'

'Fancy a trot?'

'Why not? Let's go.'

Sansara managed to sit into the movement quite comfortably while Raoul was bounced up and down like a wolf-cub on hot coals.

She had to laugh. 'I think it might be easier to canter. Just lean forward. Grip with your legs and hang on to his mane.'

'Lean forward. Grip with my legs. Hang on to the mane. Yup, I've got it.'

'Here we go, then. Follow me.'

His answer was lost to the breeze as the mare took to the straights and thundered across the plains. Raoul crouched low, gripping with his legs. The stallion could easily outpace the mare, but something kept him level. Raoul was hanging on tightly, shouting wildly and excitedly. 'This is amazing, and I haven't fallen off.'

She wanted to show him something truly magical, a place that he would never forget. A place that she had only found recently, but now could share it with someone close. Pilot knew the way, as she had been many times before. For Porter and Raoul, it was a completely new experience

The ground from here to the forest was grassland. Fallow fields and low rolling hills, high meadows and stretches of plain between them. It was safe to ride here, but Sansara still had to check on Raoul. So, as she rode, she sent out messages to the stallion, and he kept Raoul upright and in one piece.

Raoul felt empowered. He had never ridden a horse before, not even a pony. It was something his parents had never encouraged. And now here he was, riding a stallion, of all things, galloping across the land as if he had been riding forever. Beside him, Sansara rejoiced with the wind in her face and her hair flowing behind her like a rippling flame of fire.

In the distance lay her destination: looming, monstrous and imposing. That's what she was heading for. She reined back to a canter when she reached the dense perimeter and laughed out loud from the exhilaration of the gallop. Raoul caught up with her and whooped alongside her as he, too, relished the excitement. They slowed down to a walk as they entered the eaves of the forest and intuitively took note of their surroundings. And when her horse came to a halt, Sansara slid majestically off her back. Pilot billowed and snorted as she came to rest and Sansara lifted the drooping muzzle with both hands and laid her cheek on the animal's nose. Then she tucked the filly's head under her arm in a gesture of affection and offered her a handful of oats. Porter came to a halt beside them and muscled in on the free food.

'I want you to see this place. It has a magic about it.'

'You've been here before then?'

'Yes, many times. It's so beautiful here.' She breathed in the aroma and ran her palms over the soft foliage.

The glen was a small oasis, an island surrounded by trees that stood to attention like a regiment protecting the silent pool. At any time of the year, it was quiet and glistening with ripples that danced on its surface—a place where dragonflies and water boatmen skipped round the edges. Today it was more serene than ever. With an air of contentment, Sansara took Raoul's hand and strolled through a small grove of deciduous trees towards her own flowering glade—a small luxurious meadow, a verdant piece of the landscape, sitting beautifully amid the tranquil setting of the silent pool.

Here, the swathes of this year's forget-me-nots hunched dappled under the canopy of the glen, their scent still alluring, their colour mostly divine. The ruins of a crumbling monastery paid hosts to its angels where white lichen bearded the ancient granite and moss sat in clumps over the sleeping hollows. Beautiful in the day, it would take on a completely different guise at night. Sansara had leant early on that everything became different at night... if you let it.

Especially here, when the night brought chaos and disturbing images. Where giant frogs sat on the river banks guarding a pile of stones—squat, grey, menacing creatures, with huge fat throats and saucer shape eyes. Their deep guttural croaks sent out a veil of death through the arches, around crumbling windows, weaving itself over decaying buttresses and collapsed turrets. The dark lines of trees were silhouetted in the gloom, and the darkness was poised to consume if you allowed it.

Sansara only saw the beauty, no matter what time of day she rested here. For her, night brought the sound of the owl as it navigated the trees, the scamper of the fox as it scratched at the ground, and the flap of a bat as it targeted a moth. The night always had a different smell about it, and no two nights were ever the same.

She had raised the corroded candelabras and resurrected the tarnished cross. The ornate rose window was reassembled, the mullions lovingly restored. Here, the birds sang from dusk till dawn and the wind played tunes on the trees and teased her long dark braid.

He looked around in awe, taking in every particle of the islands hidden gem. Then he noticed something. 'Be very still and look over there. Near the water.' Raoul kept his voice low.

A kingfisher was hunting, poised like a statue, ready to take its meal. It didn't flinch when they came into view. It kept still, unmoving, and not once did it take its eyes off the prey. The keen observers waited as patiently as the hunter. All they could hear was the sound of their own breathing and the mewing of the buzzard overhead. Suddenly, the kingfisher darted from its perch, speared its prey, and, taking it back to its branch, knocked it senseless and swallowed the fish in one go.

'Now that's what you call impressive hunting,' said Sansara in awe of the skill.

'An expert hunter, that's what he is. And look over there, the tree creepers have formed a gymnasium of rope swings.' Raoul's face lit up at the challenge and he climbed the grassy bank to have a go on the natural-forming climber. Below him, a clear lake beckoned, its very base lined with a rich golden sediment, and water snakes slithered through the reeds. He took hold of the thick green rope, stood as far back as he was able, and catapulted himself from the highest point and landed in the water in a seated position. The water snakes slithered away, and the kingfisher darted to the other side of the pool.

She laughed at him when he surfaced with a head full of green algae.

'You look like the monster from the deep lagoon.' Her laughter was infectious.

'Perhaps I am,' he teased. 'I am the serpent from the depths of the sea.' And raising his arms high above his head, he came at her like a writhing snake. She screamed at the sight of him, scrambled up the bank and then grabbing hold of the rope, swung herself into the water. Hers was an altogether perfect entry and barely made a ripple as her body glided through the surface in a streamlined fashion. She swam back to the shore and climbed out nimbly then sat down and tilted her head back for the warmth of the sun to dry her off. Raoul came and sat down beside her and pawed at the blanket weed that was still stuck to his long hair. He couldn't help but look at her loose shirt clinging to the contours of her magnificent shape.

'You truly are a beautiful woman.'

She turned and looked at him and thought him to be the most handsome man she had ever seen with his perfect physique and tanned skin after spending hours in the outdoors. But then she looked at his grimacing face as he pulled at the green weed stuck to his head.

'Wish I could say the same about you.'

He looked at her lovingly and leaned in to kiss her. 'I know you don't mean it and that you love me really.'

The water had cooled them sufficiently on this balmy day in July. It was a magical experience, listening to the sound of crickets in the long dry grass and worker honeybees going about their day. They looked out over to the pastures where the horses were swishing away nuisance flies with their busy tails. Pilot curved her long neck down to the ground, tugging at the succulent grass. Porter was still vigilant. Even here, he kept a lookout and guarded her. Ever since the ogre had attacked her and killed their baby, he was always extra protective, but the most he saw here was a couple of leaping deer passing through the glen.

'Do you trust me?' she asked.

'Of course, I do.' he replied.

'Then close your eyes.'

With a sigh, Raoul complied. He leaned back on his elbows, the grass tickling his neck.

'What are you doing?'

He could hear her rummaging about in a bag. He still had his eyes closed but felt her move closer to him. He noticed the fresh smell first, and then a hard skin was pressed against his lips.

'What is this?' He instinctively pulled away.

'You said you'd trust me.' She tried again.

He bit into it, and a pleasant juice cracked into his mouth followed by a delicious pulp.'

'It's an apple.' He chewed the succulent fruit,

enjoying every morsel. 'What else have you got in the bag?'

'You have to guess.'

'Okay.'

'Close your eyes again.'

He locked them shut.

Something soft was put into his mouth. Something sweet and crumbly. He liked that taste.

'Cake.'

'What type of cake?'

'Cinnamon?'

'Yes. You are good at this.'

'Give me something harder to work out?'

'Okay, what about this?'

'Oh, this is easy. This is my favourite: honeyed pancakes.'

He then went on to easily guess the raisin bread and the hard-boiled eggs, and he particularly liked the new crop of sweetened lemon juice.

'Any more?'

'No, you have guessed them all.'

He smiled, then lay down on the grass and put his hands behind his head. 'This has to be the most beautiful place on earth.' He drew in a long deep breath of fresh air.

'It's my favourite place.' She leaned over to kiss the top of his head.

He reached his arm around her and pulled her close. 'If it's your favourite place, then it is mine, too.' He stroked her arm.

She felt the glow rise up from her toes, and her body

began to tingle. She lay her hand on his chest and stroked his dark, downy hairs.

'And the monastery... how long did it take you to reassemble the rose window? That's a very intricate piece of work.'

She lay in the crook of his arm, enjoying the closeness of the moment. 'I really can't recall, to be honest. I have had a lot of time on the island to fix things, remember?' She pushed a laugh through her nose in reverie.

'I love you, Sansara. You know that, don't you?' He kissed the top of her head. 'I fell in love with you the first time I saw you.'

'Love found me that day, as well.' She laced her fingers with his.

The noises of summer drifted through the glen, and she saw Pilot and Porter together in the meadow. The smell of summer had evoked a most wondrous passion.

He turned and leaned on one elbow to look at her. 'I have something for you to guess as well.'

'Really?'

'Yes, I have been meaning to do this for some time, and now seems the perfect moment.'

'Have you done some baking without me knowing.' She cocked her head sideways.

'No, but it might be just as grand.'

She smiled.

'You must close your eyes... no peeking now.'

He rummaged about in his pocket and placed two items in her hand. They were round and smooth, and she could fit her finger in the centre. She held them up to her nose but couldn't detect a smell. She brushed them across her mouth, and her sensitive lips couldn't find a flaw. They were like pieces of polished glass in her hands. They slipped on her fingers with ease and the curve of the outside edged into a flat base.

'Are they rings?'

'Yes, they are.'

She opened her eyes, and for the first time, she saw the exquisite workmanship and marvelled at the shiny black stones that he had sculpted himself.

'I made these rings a few days ago. I got up early while you were still sleeping. I found flints and abrasives in the forest then carved and rasped until I got the right finish. See how the stone shines?'

She put the smaller one on her finger and held it up to the light. 'It is exquisite, Raoul. Truly perfect.'

'The stone is born from volcanic rock. Hence, the stunning attributes.'

'Where did you find the stone?' Sansara had never before seen such a material on the island.

'When I left home to discover the outside world, my father gave me an obsidian stone for luck. He said that it is a warrior's stone that brings courage and protection to the wearer. It also stimulates the gift of prophecy.'

She gasped at the stone. 'Raoul, I don't know what to say. What a skill you have, and such a thoughtful thing to do, to carve out your gift into something that we can share.'

'Sansara... I want to share my life with you.'

She pushed out a laugh from her nose. She was thinking of something to say that was equally profound, but he continued before any words materialised.

'Will you marry me?' he blurted out.

She opened her eyes wider. She didn't know what it meant. She hadn't discussed anything like this with her sisters... or indeed, her mother. But Raoul was quite passionate about it.

'The rings are a token. A pledge of my love for you. I want you to be my wife, and I will be your husband... to cherish forever and show the Fates that we have come together as they wanted.'

She now knew that to marry someone and to be husband and wife had to be something very special. Something that came from love and devotion...and he was asking her to marry him.

'I was brought here for a reason, I survived a dreadful attack so I could be with you. We cannot disobey the Fates.'

She thought about it while he waited for her answer. This was her destiny. This is why the Fates wanted her here. She was here to save Raoul—not her father. The dream was about her and Raoul laying together, not Cornelius and his sister. She didn't have to think about it anymore. Her answer was already decided.

'Yes, of course, I will marry you.'

His happiness was ecstatic. He could hardly contain himself with excitement. 'We will be married today—right here, right now, in the monastery, by the rose window and the cross. We will be husband and wife this very day.'

'But then we will be the only ones who will know.'

'Who else needs to know, Sansara? It's only you and

me on the island... and Porter and Pilot, of course. And that's the way it's going to stay.'

'Okay. Let's do it. Let's get married.'

He picked her some flowers... the way he had seen it done back home. He knew a few of the words and knew that weddings took place in front of an altar and that you pledged yourself to the gods.

'We shall stand before the cross where we will bear witness from a higher power. I am so glad you resurrected it, because now we can receive the blessing.'

She smiled at him fondly and followed him to the sacred monument.

He positioned her on his left side and turned to face her. 'You just have to copy everything I say, so remember what I say to you.

She nodded in agreement.

Taking her bouquet and laying it down on the ground, he took her hands in his.

'Sansara, I have loved you since the moment I saw you. Your beauty and kindness have made me the happiest man alive.'

She smiled up at him.

'I will be your husband. I will always be with you, to look after you and love you, and nothing will ever alter that. Sansara will you be my wife?'

'Yes, I will.'

'Now it's your turn,' he whispered.

'Raoul, my life has taken many paths, and I have grown so much since I came to this island. But the one thing I treasure above all else is finding you. I believe you were sent here for a reason. I believe we are meant to be together and to live our lives on Tarragon Island. Raoul, there is nothing that would make me happier than to be your wife. I love you with all my heart.'

He slipped the precious stone on to her finger and kissed it, then she returned the gesture.

'Now we are man and wife. Our marriage has been sealed before the spirits. Our love has been secured with these rings. Nothing can come between us. Nothing at all.'

CHAPTER SIXTEEN

That bewitching night she spent with him was unlike anything she had experienced before. There had been a magic that evening, a dense magic she had never known existed. It wasn't the magic she felt from casting a spell or creating something with her staff—it was far more intense than that. She looked at his skin: bronzed and beautiful. The touch of his hand and the caress of his lips caused her to shudder with delight. Laying in his arms, she felt that she could take on anything; that he gave her a strength she didn't know she had. When he held her, that was the only place she wanted to be. She knew that if the Fates stopped the sea moving right then, and all the stars dropped from the sky, she would be content laying in his arms. With him, she felt that she was truly alive for the very first time. And for the first time, she embraced the peace and serenity of the island. For here, their isolation would be rewarding, and any dangers they could face together. Nothing else mattered now. Nothing at all.

. . .

The months breezed past, and the clouds obscured the sun as the wind brought the chill of autumn, and it was about this time that Raoul had a disturbing dream. He was with Sansara, walking through the ruins of the monastery. The day was calm, the air was fresh, and a halo of golden aura laced the glade.

They spotted a stag dappled in the foliage, stripping the bark off some sapling trees. Crowned with a huge rack of antlers that swayed above him, he was an impressive beast, and they took a moment to watch the animal feasting.

Though suddenly, and without warning, a figure, dressed as a hunter, leapt out and released a shaft of arrows. Each shaft flew true and pierced the stag in the chest. The beast dropped to its front legs, panting, snorting, and bellowing in a terrified panic. The arrows continued to rain down on him, the quiver never thinning of its load. Sansara broke away from Raoul and ran towards the beast, her eyes streaming tears, her voice lost in the dream, her legs slow to move. And the longer it took her to reach the injured creature, the quicker he was dying and the faster the arrows came. Another arrow, and another. They kept coming until the stag was pierced all over, and there was nothing Sansara could do. She was held back by something: a force, a mist, a mythical barrier. Try as she might, she could not break through.

Raoul reached out for her, his fingertips stretching out from every tendon and fibre in his hand. Eventually he caught her, and pulling her back, led her from the sickening scene. But Sansara was distraught. One of her flock had perished.

He woke up in a panic. He needed to check that she was safe, and as he looked over to her, he moved an errant strand of hair from her cheek and kissed her beautiful face.

He never told her about the dream for fear of alarming her unnecessarily. He didn't want to distress her. Instead he kept it to himself, for it was probably of little importance anyway.

CHAPTER SEVENTEEN

IT WAS NOW LATE OCTOBER. The nights were drawing in. The crystal water lapped at Sansara's body as she took a gentle swim before the sun went down. She had made that a daily ritual since Raoul had taught her to swim. She knew that the autumn months would bring the chill and winter quarter would bring the freeze. She wouldn't be able to swim in the lake until the following spring. Especially in her condition. She hadn't menstruated for many months, but today she felt the flutter of a new life inside her womb, and with it came the overwhelming love for her unborn child. She gently rubbed her belly and started to hum. *Do babies feel anxiety at this early stage? Have they got the capacity to feel distressed?* She hoped not but continued to hum a gentle song just in case. She would have to make a new dress for herself, she decided. Her present ones would not withstand her widening girth as it was. She chuckled as she remembered the size the gestating sows got to, the ewes as well, but that didn't worry her. Raoul's happiness and her baby's safety were paramount in her mind. She remembered how happy he was when she had told him. He swung her round in delight and lifted her into the air.

'I will love you forever, Sansara. You know that, don't you?'

'Of course, I do, and I will love you for eternity.'

The merriment played over in her mind as she remembered the happiest moment of her life. They had shared so many wonderful experiences together, all in less than a year. Swimming, horse riding, walking, talking, and sharing the day together. But now, expecting a baby together, well, that was truly magical. Her thoughts turned to images of her mother and her sisters. What a day that would be when she ventured back to her childhood home and shared her news, and they finally met her handsome husband. She could barely contain the excitement and couldn't wait to tell her mother that she had been mistaken. The Fates had given her Raoul for all her endeavours on the island. It was Raoul calling for help. It was him she had to save. Her mother had been wrong all those years ago. She had been confused. She had seen the wrong man, heard the wrong voice. It was Raoul calling for help, not her father in another dimension somewhere. She had thought about it often, how impossible that would be. Travelling through time and saving a man who was just barely a few years older than her. No, the wrong prophecy was spoken. In another five months, she would have been on the island for five years. What an exorbitant amount of time to have waited, she thought. She stopped. All this thinking about what might have been or what should have been...it didn't matter now. The past seven months had been shared with Raoul. That made up for everything. Her loneliness, her isolation. Even Pilot hadn't been around since her wedding day. *Where has she got to?* But Raoul had been the making of her. Nothing compared to him. Nothing else mattered now.

She heard an animal bark in the distance. She saw the sun wink on the surface of the lake. That made her smile.

But was it the sun winking? Was it an animal barking? The next minute, her world transformed into one of flame and smoke. The trees in the glade were like pillars of burning fires, sending out showers of sparks and debris into the water. A herd of deer sprang through the woods, their flamed white tips bobbing in the shadows. Birds took to the air, flying low, as plumes of smoke rose up into waves of streaky grey. They were all making for the sea, though. Sansara had to go in the opposite direction. To be with Raoul. To get her staff.

She soaked her woollen robe and threw it over her sodden hair. It should give her some protection as she ran through the fire. Then emptying her pitcher of eggs, she refilled it with water and submerged her head scarf—it was all she could think of to help with the treacherous journey back. She took flight on the ground, skimming through the undergrowth and jumping over roots and fallen tree limbs.

'Hang on in there little one—this is going to be a bumpy ride.'

The heat was unbearable, but the smoke was worse. Choking, she covered her mouth with the scarf, grateful for the wetness and protection. Still she ran, her legs aching already from the climb, her arms barely able to carry the pitcher. The smoke was creeping through the trees, obscuring her view, so at every turn, she was slapped, torn, or gashed from a stricken bough spiralling in the haze.

Into open land, she staggered up the path. Animals that she had never seen before were not bothered by her appearance—the fire was their enemy right now. They flocked past her in their droves. She hurdled over a burning log and almost fell but managed to skim it safely. Her throat continued to burn, and her lungs felt as though they were on fire. She doused herself with water and swilled the charcoal residue from her mouth. Trembling from exhaustion and with very little oxygen, tears began to fall. 'Raoul, where are you? Please help me.'

A piercing scream cut through the brume like a butcher's blade. She shuddered and staggered onwards.

A fireball hurtled over her and knocked another tree to its doom. It was becoming perilous now, and she feared for her life. The air was dark with soot, and ash was spreading like snow, but she was going by instinct now rather than sight. Another dousing of water cleared her eyes temporarily. It was still black. She had to keep going. Suddenly her thoughts turned to Pilot and the herd. She begged the higher powers for them to be safe. They did have the advantage of speed, though, plus their sharper instincts, of course. 'Please be safe,' she heard herself whisper.

A smell of singeing hair quickly erased those thoughts from her mind. *Where's that smell coming from?* And then the searing pain came. She threw the pitcher of water over her before her whole head caught fire. The sizzle from the extinguished strands was barely audible against the chaos of the devastation. With stinging eyes, she limped on, forcing herself to take small breaths between pursed lips. She had no water now. But she knew she must be nearly home. Then she caught sight of her shelter, but not before she saw Raoul lying face down on the ground. A collapsed tree was burning at his side. The wound to his back was brutal.

Running to him, she sank by his side and stroked his head. He did not respond. A gash to his temple was severe. The injury to his back was gaping. Charred black flesh had burned right down to the bone. His ribs were exposed, broken and caved in. His muscles had disintegrated.

She screamed once, twice, maybe more, she lost count. But her voice was not heard above the wrath of the flames. The fire consumed without hesitation and torched everything into a morass of devastation around her. Sobbing, she dragged him in to the shelter and onto their palette. She grabbed her wand and shouted out a spell to create a dome that would keep them safe. Then, viewing the awesome spectacle, she hovered it over his broken body. Nothing happened. She cast a command over him. Still nothing. She touched him with the tip of the wand but his wounds remained smouldering. The smell of burning flesh made her nauseous.

All the time wasted minutes were ticking by. The wand was discarded. She assembled her herbs and spices, heated up some water, and prepared a moly. She collected her materials and spoke to him continually.

'Come back to me, Raoul. Come back. I can heal you, just like I did before. Do you remember? All those months ago. Nothing can part us, remember? Nothing at all. And now we have a baby—she grows in my belly—yours and mine. From our seeds... they have become one. I felt her today. She moves, Raoul. I can feel her beating heart. Please, Raoul, please say something. Anything.'

He remained silent.

Gently, she washed his face with an absorbent piece of rabbit skin dipped in a simmering liquid of boiled iris root. Then, she scooped out the root pulp, and put it directly on his wound, covering the unguent with the same piece of rabbit skin. All the time she was humming and chanting, telling him to come back to her, urging him to stay strong. A soft downy robe was draped over his shoulders and a vial of moly and yarrow was given to him orally.

'You are not going to die, my dear Raoul. I can bring you back to life. I am not going to lose you. Do you hear me?'

She cut away the remains of his shirt and flushed out the charcoal and splinters from the crater in his back. She washed the wound with an infusion of bugloss and astringent from the simmering cauldron. She called his name constantly.

He did not respond.

He did not move.

His body was getting colder.

Still she worked.

Under the gaping hole, she could see the torn muscles and seared tendons, so she quickly went over to her store of medicines and poured the ground up leaves of lady's mantle that would cauterize them. When she was satisfied with the result, she took a needle made of splintered bone and a strand of wet sinew from a pot of moist snapdragon weed and began to sew it all back together. She put twenty-eight knots along the wound and covered it all with a poultice from the mashed iris root. Covering him with a thicker blanket, she then went to get a vial of pure comfrey oil which she sprinkled on the palette.

'Raoul, can you hear me? Breathe in the comfrey oil, it will make you better. Just like before. You are safe now, I have fixed you. I have used my powers to heal you and bring you back from the dead.'

He didn't respond. The room was silent.

She lit a candle, so the darkness didn't consume him. She needed to watch him and wait for the steady rise and fall of his chest. The candle burned. The wax melted. Soon it was a solid pool in its diminishing container. She watched as a moth fluttered towards the flame. Lured by the light, it risked its life. *Why do they do that?* she wondered *Why are they drawn to something that is so dangerous?* Maybe it's something in another time that guides them.

The thought tired her. Her knees ached on the cold, wooden floor. She felt her neck stretching and snapping as she defied the call to sleep. Reluctantly, she gave in, and laying down next to him, held him close to keep him warm.

. . .

Dawn came with hazy grey skies and an air that burned the soul. She came to her senses slowly, a dim light penetrating the grey blur of slumber. She opened one of her sleep-deprived eyes. The air smelled of rain, and the heavy clouds had burst into a monsoon. Through the shutters, little drops seeped through and landed on her tear-stained cheeks. She wiped them away and opened the other gritted eye. *Thank goodness for rain* she thought. She rolled over and felt something wet between her legs as she moved. At first, she thought it was the rain water, but her hand told her it was blood. She fought back the scream and watched the liquid run down her fingers. She looked over to Raoul. He was still. She touched him with her bloodied hand. Tears welled into pools of despair and tumbled on to his pallid face.

Outside was a smoking wasteland. The fire had largely burned itself out with the rain, but here and there a few patches were still smouldering. The forest was a mass of blackened spears thrust into the sky. Other trees had fallen and lay charred and broken, their hearts had extinguished hours ago. The flies and maggots were already hard at work on the animal carcasses. A veil of death obscured the sun.

Her wails went on for days. She only went outside to stand in the rain and wash the death from her body. Her skin was covered in wood-smoke and blood. Her blood, Raoul's blood, her baby's blood, all mixed together in a sickening concoction of failure and loss.

'Why?' she screamed to the skies. 'Why do you punish me so? Haven't I served you enough? Haven't I faced every challenge you threw at me with strength and fortitude? Haven't I embraced everything on this island? Obviously, I am not good enough. I got it wrong. I have failed you, and that's why you took both my loves away. That's why you tore them from my breast in the cruellest way possible—because I am not good enough for you. Well, I give in. I am not worthy of you, and so I am walking away. My father will have to die like my child, like my husband. I cannot save him. I could not save my dearest Raoul, nor could I carry my beautiful baby, so why should I save my father? Why should he live? Tell me that 'o' great one that doesn't speak. Tell me that?'

NOTHING CAME BACK AT HER.
Her questions remained unanswered.
It was silent.

'I AM RETURNING to my mother and my sisters. I am going back to them. And if you want me to give my life to the great wrath of the sea, then you will have to fight me for that as well. Do you hear me? Do you hear me?' Her voice carried the weight of a thousand gales.

THERE WAS NOTHING.
It was still.
It was quiet.

'I AM LEAVING this place of death. But I will leave you

with the ghosts and the burial mounds. I will leave you with the memories of happier times, of laughter and hope and dreams. For somewhere in one of your worlds, my daughter walks with her father. Pilot walks with her Porter. Maybe they are all together. But I am leaving this place. I will never return. Do you hear me?'

SHE WAS IGNORED.
No reasons given.
She was left blind to the cause.

SHE BURIED her husband on the mound and erected a plaque for him. *Dearest Raoul*. She spent days making a beautiful casket for their baby, embellished with sea shells and adorned with pearls. *Our daughter Delphine*.

The casket was placed next to her husband, overlooking the tranquil lake and the hypnotic sea. The place they spent so often together. The place where their baby was conceived. She didn't want to stay here anymore. She wanted to go home to her mother and her sisters. She had lost everything now. Nothing was worth staying for. She packed her small bag, carried her staff, and left the shelter for the very last time.

CHAPTER EIGHTEEN

Behind her, the pale circle of sun glowed above the burial mound, casting shadows on their graves. She wiped away a tear and sighing heavily, climbed up the ladder to her vessel. Sansara raised the mainsail and took her place at the helm—the island fell away as the ship surged ahead and made for the open sea. She passed a small inlet where the leatherback turtles were laying their eggs. She smiled at how peaceful it was and how they always returned to the same place to spawn. It reminded her of home, and she set the boat to top speed.

Once she was beyond the protection of the bays, the weather began to change. The clouds rose up like black mountains behind her, their summits alive with blue and purple lightning. The swells grew so voraciously that the ship slid down the back of each wave and rode high on the next one. The sea was lead-grey beneath a granite sky, and the coastline slid by unnoticed in a veil of mist.

But she weathered that storm with ease and let out a triumphant yell. She kept her eyes fixed on the prow.

Unwavering, unfeeling, nothing more could break her now. She didn't care what *'they'* threw at her now. She didn't sleep. She didn't eat. The cruel way her life had unfolded lay in ruins around her. She felt like she was seven hundred years old. Though she didn't care too much for age or life now—she was nearly broken.

On the third day, the weather turned stormy again and this time bitterly cold. The rigging crackled and the sea hissed, but still she held her position. With the wind and tide behind her, the ship flew through the ocean passage, yawning and shuddering as she was gripped by the riptides. Icy spray flew up like daggers and tried to pierce her skin. Sansara immediately pulled her cloak in tighter and vented her wrath.

'Go on, keep bombarding me. Try to finish me off. Do you want me to fall even further? Do you want the sea to claim me?' Her words were lost to the wind. 'Well you can't have me—you can't have all of me.'

A snap of lightning hit the mainsail and split it in two. A crack of thunder shuddered through the deck. Ocean spray surged over the hull. The sea grew rougher and the winds howled, pushing the ship down, then whipping round to the stern and forcing her back up on her haunches again. Gallons of sea and rain water deluged the ship's frame, soaking any crevasse or unattended door. Time and again, the ship was thrashed about like a pawn in a tidal wave. The wind never waned and the sea never tired. Nothing was as strong and fierce as an angry storm.

Except Sansara.

The wind tore at her face, half blinding her with its

ferocity, every patch of exposed skin was stinging, and every hair follicle was standing on its end. Still, she gripped the helm. Her hair hung like reeds, her wet clothes clung to her like a second skin. Her hands were red raw and bleeding, her spirit clinging on like a drowning man.

She heard the sound of someone screaming, then she realised it was her own voice, shouting at the Fates, determined that they would not take her down to the depths of the ocean. Her wrath raged like the storm. Neither would yield. The sea grew rougher and the wind created small tornadoes, whipping up everything in its path. It took her staff and tossed it into the waves. Lightning bolts shimmered across the sea, lighting up the enormity of her challenge.

Still she held on. Still she would not give in.

The storm raged on. The wind had now gained greater force from her staff. For the first time, she felt powerless. Her situation seemed hopeless. She had to concede.

But not yet.

A shrieking rise of power rushed into her path, knocking her against the hull. She gulped in deep breaths as she slid down against the wooden struts. Where the sea had failed, another force took over. Raw energy flooded her sacred centres of power—opening, pushing, seeking. Her head was spinning. Her core was burning. A different kind of strength pulsed through her veins. She had released her energy. She looked up and a dragon was in front of her, rearing on the cliff, obscuring a smaller dragon. The dragon's legs slammed down onto the precipice and two sets of long sapphire claws grabbed the edge and sliced into the stone. Fragments of rock showered down, sending up clouds of rain-covered dust over the ship. Her leathery wings spread for balance as she ducked her head and roared. The gale was forced to yield. The rain trembled in its wake and ceased its bombardment. The wind turned to a gentle warm breath, tingeing Sansara's mouth with wild orchids and sweet cinnamon. The sea was calm, the sun pierced the clouds with her golden rays, and a thousand fledgling fireflies took to the mountains.

Forests of blue seaweed grew up from the depths, waving at the sun like tall pines in a breeze. Beds of recumbent shells were arranged into beautiful gardens, embellished with fingers of sea anemone and antlers of coral. Schools of fish darted in and out of the underground city, turning it gold, then silver, then back to blue again. A pallid light turned everything translucent, where shimmering jellyfish floated through time like a living constellation, and purple threads hung in drools from their bodies, skirting the coral with ease.

Sansara watched the delicate landscape unfold, and suddenly felt cleansed and refreshed like the sea. She felt ignited with intensity. She had been reborn. And with the dragon's huge head lowering ever closer to her own, Sansara was not afraid, for this was a kindred spirit born from the flames of mankind, sent to resurrect the souls of the innocent.

Delicately, the dragon lowered her muzzle and showed Sansara the Sapphire of the Sorceress, a stone so precious that it held, within its core, the stories of the innocents spanning a thousand years—of their rise and fall, of their wisdom and sovereignty, of their very creation and purpose. The dragon breathed out flames of red and gold that flicked across the young sorceress and turned the ship into a burning pyre of embers. The smaller dragon swept in with enormous talons and lifted Sansara from the vessel and carried her back to the shelter on her island.

Sansara had a restless night. She tossed and turned. Fighting dragons and wild beasts, battling the wind and rain, conquering fires and total annihilation. She felt the sweat pour off her as if she was shedding a second skin, and in its place came power and glory, followed by a sense of well-being. A voice came to her as she slept. A comforting reassuring tone that pacified her.

'You have not failed us, daughter of Mawi. You have not angered the spirits. We favour you. We need you. Raoul and Delphine are not lost to you. We have only borrowed them. You will be reunited one day. That is our word. Hold that thought that as you complete your tasks.'

In her sleep, the words were like a moment of pleasure. It was a relief to feel something other than relentless grief and loss.

As a cool blue dawn broke over her island, Sansara opened her eyes. She was warm and the candlelight was golden. There were fur robes on her bed. Glass panes in the windows. The fire was crackling. She detected different smells of camphor sweetened by the rich honey of wood wax, of orchids and cinnamon. Everywhere seemed to be red velvet and rich blue satin. She made a low noise in the back of her throat and attempted to get up. But she fell back when her aching muscles wouldn't let her.

She looked around. This was not the same shack that she had left a few days previously. Now it was an enormous building of marble and alabaster. A jug of crystal water was next to her bed with a vial of blue liquid. She mixed them together and instantly felt revived when she swallowed it. Her brown hessian tunics were nowhere to be seen. Though she felt the lightest fabric over her shoulders—a close silk weave gown that felt like a whisper against her skin with seven embroidered emperor moths worked along the hemline and sash ends edged with lapis tassels. Hanging on a clothes stand was midnight blue tunic with silver embroideries, girdled by a sash of delicate lace. In addition, there were several other robes of luxurious weave that pooled to the floor in a tapestry of wealth.

She walked down the long corridors that lead off to brand new rooms. Lush blue carpets lay underfoot, expensive hangings adorned the walls. Carved lapis stood in niches, silk cushions lay under windows. *What had happened to her? She could only recall climbing into the ship to return home, and then her mind went blank.*

The kitchen was long and brimming with food: cabbage tossed with nuts, duck with beans, cold eggs with mustard, pickled vegetables and salads, greens dressed in oils, rice rolled in seaweed and round pea cakes served with ginger. Herbs and plants lay ready prepared on the huge oak worktable. And through the arch of a brand-new courtyard, she saw a well-stocked garden edged in silver from the morning sun. She followed the path to face a carefully-laid-out garden with narrow paths winding around flowerbeds, miniature trees adorned with birds, and a wooden bridge arched over a golden pond that rippled to the tune of orange carp.

But what came next truly took her breath away, for coming through the shadows of a path lined with blossom trees, were her two friends, Pilot and Porter. They had not died in the fire, they had not perished as Sansara supposed. Pilot whinnied and came trotting up. But more precious than that was the sight of a new foal, a black and white colt. That's where she had gone. She had returned home to be with the sire and bring a new leader into the world. Sansara ran out and wreathed her arms around the mare's neck. She stroked the baby. Porter stood guard—as always. The clouds broke, the sun shone, and glinting round Pilot's neck was a brilliant blue pendant so pure that even if the sun had not been out, it would have lit up the island with its voluminous beams. She took it in her hands and peered into the rotating orb. Clouds of images graced the iridescent sphere, and it became a living organism circling in her hands. She could see it all, past and present. Her father's life and her own life. Every path was moving with joy and pain, happiness and sorrow, life and death as the years moved forward.

She also saw the future and held it to her heart. She felt a warm tear run down her cheek. The message that she heard last night was written. Images of her family were shown. A woman with the emperor moth emblazoned on her back crusaded through the orb. Another bearing the insignia of the moth strode through after her. These were important women, and ones which she had yet to serve amongst many others, of that she was certain.

This was the sapphire jewel of power. The stone that meant she had passed all the tests—the Sapphire of the Sorceress. This was what she had been striving for, waiting for, praying for, nearly died for. And now she knew it was time. She sighed contentedly and looked up to the skies. A shard of light turned the gnarled old staff golden and placed it at her feet. The island would never suffer to the elements, or anything else, again.

Sansara walked through her sprawling new home with pride. Never before had she felt so empowered. Ahead, sunlight blazed off the mountain range, sending a shiver down her spine. She didn't feel small in its presence anymore, she didn't feel dwarfed by its magnitude. Her head was held high. She wore the stone of power around her neck and carried the golden staff.

Then, she heard it. She heard her name, someone was calling her. A young man, he was frightened, but surrounded by loved ones. The prophecy from her mother had come true—the totem of a stag had slain her father, but she had the power to save him. For he was the reason that she lived. But according to the orb, she had one or two other matters to attend to first.

CHAPTER NINETEEN

Hailing the blue dragon, she stood on the mound dressed in a long gown of azure blue. A cloak billowed from her shoulders in a haze of silver gauze, and her long black hair flared out behind her like a burning flame of smoke. Sansara was ready for her mission. The blue dragon swept in and crouched down low. The light of the sun glittered off her scales as tendrils of white smoke filtered from between her teeth. Her eyes were yellow with black vertical pupils to help her distinguish between light and darkness. Her horns were pure lapis lazuli, and the claws on her feet shone like jewels. She lifted Sansara to the nape of her neck and launched them both into the sky, blasting through the clouds, and cutting the air with huge seraph wings. Down below was a blush of meadows and forests, lakes and sea. For a long time, it blurred into grey mist everywhere where the sun had been swallowed by time and the worlds were separated by gloom. But then the umbra consumed them, and she had to rely on her dragon's phenomenal sight as they navigated time.

. . .

SHE KNEW she was nearing her destination when the colours turned from black to blue to green again, and the landscape became awash in colour. Further ahead was the fortified bulwark with crenellated walls and towers at each corner. A light summer rain was falling, and the dragon turned her blue scales silver to blend in with the clouds. Then, lowering Sansara onto the wall-walk, she turned on a wing and took to the mountains. Sansara looked into the orb to determine her route. Her light silver cloak was pulled high to give her invisibility. With hushed, undetectable steps she descended to the pit of the mountain where the coals were smouldering black, orange, and red.

'Give me time to complete this task, flame of life. Allow me permission to save those whom have saved my father.' She heard the rumble in its bowels. 'When I am away from here, you can ignite your doom. This place will cease to be, and any living creature contained within its walls will rot in the depths of the underworld forever.' The flames roared and she held out the orb.

Narrowing her eyes and taking a deep breath, she plunged deep into the stone of the sorceress. Blue energy exploded through her, and she heard the fire respond. She felt the power in her veins, rushing through her blood, and the force of a thousand witches surged forward with a torrent of blue energy that roared with ancient annihilation. The flames had revealed the course of her task.

First came the prisoners, freed by her father. She had

to assist them in the dark labyrinths of the mine. Curling through the twisted maze, she found them edging through the labyrinth, many in a state of shock, all in disbelief.

It was dark all the way through, but a lantern offered some sort of comfort. The men were feeling their way deeper into the cave, a vast expanse of tunnels and chambers running in all directions.

The men couldn't see much at all, but sensed they were going deeper, and so far down that they must have been miles beneath the mountain now. It became damp and cold. They had to crawl on their hands and knees, and then down onto their bellies.

These men had all pledged allegiance to Cornelius. They had saved him and manufactured his redemption. They would need a protective spell to guide them home. She breathed her magic over their safety and ensured that the route was marked with pointers and the path would glow with light. Restoring the mud pool, there would be a spring of fresh water at the end of their escape, and three sturdy reinforced boats replaced the old worn ones tethered to a rock. Then a protective dome was arched over their homeward bound journey, so they would not perish when the mountain blew.

She saw the gunpowder in a spidery vein that lead back up to the upper chambers. Following it, she entered the room of death, but was not prepared for the sheer number of men for there were scores and scores of soldiers. She could smell the sour stink of their anticipation like the reek of caged animals. The avidity in their faces was brutal. These men wanted to inflict pain, they wanted to see death, and they would not rest until their swords dripped with the blood of innocents. They all had to go.

Then she saw the young woman in a wedding dress. Her face bore a look of terror, her eyes wide like a startled doe. Her hair hung loose over her shoulders, and her hands were clasped to her chest, concealing a razor-sharp weapon on the inside of her sleeve.

What can I do against hundreds of men eager for blood? Sansara heard her thought.'

The king was addressing Saskia now:

Don't you think you are lucky, to live a life of ease with everything at your fingertips? You can have anything you want. Anything at all. I can give it to you.' He looked over her shoulder. 'All of these people around you, all of them, are here to offer you a service.'

She nodded meekly again. Her blood chilled at the thought of them working to please her.

'I offered someone else that once, you know.'

The air froze. His eyes narrowed.

'Someone very close to me.'

He stepped forward and moved to the open window. The bird flapped its wings. Hooded, blinded, tethered. Like everyone else in the room, it wanted to fly away and be free. The king breathed in the air and looked towards the mountains. The sun drenched the horizon, and the warmth poured through the window, spilling into every nook and every crevasse. But it was still cold in the hall. Nothing could make it warm.

Saskia chewed on her bottom lip.

Cornelius kept an eye on the guards.

'I loved this person with all my heart,' he continued. 'I gave them everything.'

He turned and walked towards Saskia. He faced her again.

'I am so sorry that I have to do this on our wedding day. But it's such an important day for me—for us—and I want to start afresh, anew, with no doubts at all. You do understand, don't you, Saskia?'

She nodded.

'Speak, girl, speak. Only the fearful stay silent. Only the coward nods his head. Only the traitor remains mute.'

She quickly stammered her answer. 'Yes, I understand, my lord. I understand everything.'

'It's all about trust, Saskia. It's all about respect and honesty. Can you see that?'

She was trying hard to calm her nerves, fearful that he could see right through her now. She nodded again.

'Yes, I can see that.'

The king smiled at her. A sickly, meaningless smile. His eyes narrowed. He licked his lips—slowly. Her legs nearly buckled beneath her with fear. He spun on his heels and withdrew his dagger. With perfect aim, he threw it at Coben's neck. The knife hit him in the throat, sinking up to its hilt. His shout became a wet gurgle as he clutched the blade.

'No!' Saskia cried out.

The maids screamed. The musicians couldn't believe what they had just seen. The soprano fainted. Two guards stepped forward to hold Saskia.

Coben was still alive.

The king gritted his teeth. His nostrils flared in anger. He raged to within an inch of his brother's face.

'I know what you have been doing. Do you think I am stupid? Do you think I am an imbecile?'

His brother was on his knees now, clutching the blade. Saskia was trying to break free of the guards.

'Always trying to get one over on me. I gave you everything. I took you in when you had nothing. I gave you a home.'

'Brother...' Coben's voice was weak.

'Brother?' Saskia creased her face in shock.

'I know that it was you who let that prisoner go. I know you got a horse. I know you helped him.'

Coben was on the floor, covered in blood. But still the wrath of the king continued.

'You betrayed me, ...and this is what happens to those who betray.'

Atilus was marched forward.

Saskia stood rigid, rooted to the spot. Why was Atilus here?

The king stood up. He wiped the sweat from his brow and straightened his apparel. 'Ah, young man. How have you liked your time in the iron rooms?'

Atilus struggled and tried to shout out, but the tight wadding around his mouth stopped his frantic words.

'Now, now, two months is nothing compared to what other traitors have had.' The sinister smile spread across the king's face.

Coben was still hanging on to the blade. If he took

it out now, the blood would flow. But Segan wanted him alive for just a bit longer. To hear everything that he had to say.

'This little guy told me what you did.' The king looked at the bedraggled boy, tethered, bound, gagged.

'He betrayed his family for freedom.' Hezekiah cocked his head and sneered at the trembling figure before him. Then looked down at Coben.

'I don't like traitors. I don't like people who betray family for their own ends.'

His sword went straight through the young lad's body. Atilus crumpled to the floor and died instantly. Hezekiah then sucked the sword out of the corpse and plunged it into his brother.

She thought of Vlavos. She saw him dying at the hands of the blade. She thought of Coben, she had grown to love him like a father. She screamed again. The power surged through her veins. She roared like a warrior summoning all the strength she had.

The king turned round, shocked, aghast. He wasn't expecting this from a woman. His mouth was wide open in bewilderment. She broke free of her constraints, and in a blur of speed, she withdrew her knife and plunged it into Hezekiah's heart. Then she swung round and sliced the jugular of the guards behind her.

Sansara heard the whimpering. The fierce yells and shrill screams. It all had to end. When the king was slain, the demons bellowed and surged. But Sansara's sceptre blocked the way, and they all fell where they stood, taking their death and decay with them into a pile of molten ash. Cornelius was quick to react, for he had already worked out his line of attack and slit the throat of a guard with his back to him. He retrieved the sword quickly as another guard ran up to him. Cornelius faced the assailant, keeping his weapon locked in front of him. The sword was scarred with use, the edges splintered. The guard made the first move, yelling as he charged. Cornelius avoided the first strike, but the guard pressed in to the attack, forcing him back with a series of short cutting blows. Cornelius recovered his stance and they crashed together. Swords locked, hilts engaged, neither one ready to yield. Cornelius snarled and shoved his blade forward. The guard fell, his grip gone. With a quick, stiff-armed strike, Cornelius smacked the sword from his hand, sending it flying, and as the guard sprawled on his back, Cornelius stood over him, pointing the tip of the blade at his throat. The deed was done quickly.

Another guard came at him, but he was soon disposed of. In the blink of an eye, Cornelius had vaulted onto a table with a dagger in his hand, and sprinting down the surface, kicked the bowls and plates of food everywhere. Someone made a grab for his leg, but he kicked them unconscious. Another aimed a bow, but that was punched out of the way. He wrestled another off the bench.

Saskia ducked as a sweep cut nearly took her in the neck. She parried her attacker, locking the man's blade into her own hilt, then threw back her head and gave a long, loud roar that pulsed through the room and shocked her attacker into submission. A perfectly aimed swipe downwards ended his life. She then went on to hack a pathway through the dozen or so soldiers in front of her.

Cornelius drove his blade into the chest of another soldier and pulled the sword free, kicking the dying man out of the way. Another soldier came from the left, head down, straight into his ribs. The wind was knocked out of him and a low tackle took them crashing into the plinth of the falcon. The leather book spun into the air and landed by Cornelius. The bird, still tethered and hooded, squawked in fear. The attacker was on top of Cornelius, his face was sickly and desperate, as he repeatedly rammed Cornelius' head on the floor. Cornelius heard the sound of sliding metal and a dagger appeared at his side. Saskia willed the life back into him from the sidelines. Cornelius grabbed the dagger and plunged it into the side of the assailant.

When a guard drew two swords against Cornelius, it was then that Sansara could see inside his head, struggling to make sense of what had happened to him. His mind was elsewhere. She had to help him, so she sent the two swords to impale themselves on two more attacking guards. A dagger found its way into the lone soldier's throat. Another sword hissed through the air like a scythe, sweeping the heads off a battalion running towards Saskia. A lethal swing deflected another vicious blow, and the guard fell back on a pool of blood, taking another five with him as they landed heavily on the stone paving littered with a regiment of arrows. Still the carnage continued, still Cornelius struggled with his demons. Sansara thwarted another unsuccessful attempt to slay him, then she heard Saskia call his name.

Saskia had already pushed her way into the heart of the fighting when Cornelius came out of his trance. Around them, officers were marshalling their men back into ranks with roared orders and the butts of their swords. The arch was thick with panicked men, some surging through the corridors, others being driven back by blades hissing through the air. She watched as Saskia flipped in the air and took out three guards: one with her heel, one with her sword, and another with her dagger. All collapsed to the ground. The sour release of urine mixed with the coppery stink of fresh blood congealed on the slippery floor.

With Cornelius and Saskia in control, Sansara heard the sucking gurgle of Coben's breath and leapt towards him.

'Goddess, help me.' His words brushed her over like a prayer, and an aura of silver thread held him in a death-like state. She felt his pain and removed it. She felt the fear of never seeing his daughter again, and she removed that as well. Her staff protected him as the battle scene came to a gradual halt. Saskia knelt beside him and thanked him for everything he had done. Atilus was further insulted with the wrath of her sword.

Sansara looked down at Atilus lying in a pool of blood, damning him with a blank stare. *Too young and too stupid* she thought to herself. But he would grow into a coward and an informant if he lived. He had already caused the *'death'* of Coben, and there would be many more to follow if she lifted the veil. No, he had to stay here and perish with the rest of the usurpers.

It wouldn't be long now.

Waiting for Saskia and Cornelius to make their exit, she grabbed the dying man, and with the wrath of the flames within her, lifted him into the air. She heard the approach of a small animal racing through the cogs of the mine—it was frightened and agitated. Seeing her master, she started barking. A pointed finger calmed her immediately.

Within seconds, a scroll was gently secured in her jaw, and Digger was on her way to Aiden Hall. Moira would learn of Coben's whereabouts within the hour.

'Goddess, make for the gate,' Coben spurted, as the rumble came from below.

'I am taking you further than the gate.' She replied.

Her sceptre formed a protective shield as she lifted him higher into the air, and the blue dragon swooped in to take them on their journey.

A wind caressed his face and raked his hair.

'I am not afraid,' she heard him say. *'I have redeemed the errors of my ways, and now I earn the right to happiness.'*

CHAPTER TWENTY

This dragon wouldn't take long to reach her destination with outstretched wings that glided through time. The cloudy blue scales of her underbelly shimmered in the noon sky, and the sun turned her dorsal scales silver as she dipped in and out of the clouds. When she dropped her massive head to align with her body, the magnificent tail propelled them to an even greater speed. Sansara leaned forward to take hold of the golden horns. Coben followed her lead with his thick arms around her waist.

Sansara turned her head to speak with him. 'I know you might find this hard to believe, Coben, but I have come to reunite you with your daughter.'

'How? That's impossible.'

'Is it? So, in your life you have learned about everything that is possible and impossible?'

'I hadn't really thought about it very much.' His stammered answer was empty.

'I have to tell you that we live in a world where everything is decided by what we can see and touch. If we can't see it or we don't understand it, then it doesn't exist.' Sansara repeated her mother's words. 'What if I told you that what may seem impossible here, is, in fact, highly probable in another world.'

His expression was incredulous.

'And quite possibly, that other world might choose you to do something that must be done.'

'What must I do?' he asked in bewilderment.

'It's not what you must do, it's what you have already done. You saved a lot of people. You saved my father. You saved a sister, a kindred spirit of mine, one who wears the insignia of the moth.'

'Saskia?'

'Yes, Saskia, and she now loves my father, whom you also saved, and they will go on to do good things together. And it's all because you are a chosen one.'

Coben frowned behind her in disbelief.

'Don't disbelieve what is right in front of you, Coben. You must believe it exists. And now you will be reunited with your daughter, Lace, for she has missed you.'

Coben felt the warm tear run down his cold cheek.

'And then you will be reunited again with Moira, for she weeps for your safety.'

'Goddess, I cannot thank you enough.'

'I have sent a message to Moira via your faithful Digger. The message would have reached her by now. And here is an invitation for you, and it's not to be read until you have spoken with Lace.'

The parchment was secured in his pocket with a reassuring pat. 'Not to be opened until I am alone. I give you my word.'

Sansara smiled, pleased that her mission was going smoothly. The dragon accelerated and set her course to the far north, home of the Marshland Tribe.

Moira was chatting to Troubadour, the family hound. She had just spoken with Master Philipe about Coben's position at Aiden Hall. Coben had been right—he had been offered work. Troubadour followed her to an old discarded log and sat down at her feet while she looked out yonder.

'Dearest Troubadour, are you happy now that everyone is reunited?'

The dog looked up at her with big soulful eyes. Moira stroked his head.

'Look at everyone, Troubadour. See how happy they all are. The Mistress and the Master are together again, and look at Tiller and Winta, they are planning a Yuletide wedding. How wonderful that will be. I will bake a cake and there will be so much merriment in the house again. But alas, our Asher will be gone soon to live a life as a squire's wife at Condor Vale.'

She chuckled to herself. 'Who'd have thought it, eh, Trouby? Our Asher going to live at Condor Vale with His Lordship and Her Ladyship.'

She was lost in thought as she smiled on the reunited couples, and then returned to her conversation with Troubadour.

'But I have a secret, Trouby. Do you want to know what it is?'

The dog looked up at her and pawed at her hand.

'I'll tell you my secret, if you really want to know.' She leaned in closer to the dog and almost whispered. 'I have also found love.' She looked around to make sure no one was listening. 'Do you believe me, Trouby? Of course, you do. I fell in love as well. During those darkest hours, those most frightening of times, through truly difficult days, I found love in the most unlikeliest of places.'

She smiled at the thought and remembered the way Coben looked at her, the way he had brushed her face and touched her hand. She let out a breathy laugh. 'And he will come back to me. I know he will. He's just got to find a way home with Saskia; because he is strong and brave, courageous and loyal. When he returns to me, we will be together, like the Mistress and the Master, like Tiller and Winta, like Squire Dom and Asher. It will be Coben and Moira, and it will be us walking down the aisle to a new life together.'

She looked down at the dog and stroked his head. 'Shall I tell you something else, Trouby?'

The dog seemed to understand every word she was saying.

'This is the first time I have ever been in love—truly in love.' She took in a deep breath of air and let it out slowly. 'And he loves me, Trouby. He does, he really does. And for the first time in my life, I am truly happy.'

She looked out yonder, hoping to see Coben come round the corner as he did so often at Hezekiah Hall. She missed him so much and felt a warm tear run down her face. She wiped it away, knowing that he would be okay. He was a man of high standing; a soldier, a guard. Of course, he would be okay.

Then her thoughts turned to Atilus. Where was he, she wondered? Tiller was the hot-headed one, liable to something impulsive. Atilus was the more sensible of the two and wouldn't do anything stupid. She puffed out her cheeks in frustration and shook her head.

'I hope he hasn't done anything foolish, Troubadour. I don't know what he could have done, but, really, he should be here by now.'

She looked into the woeful eyes again. 'Do you know where he is, Trouby? Has he taken a wrong turn? Has he lost his way?' She let out a big sigh. 'Well this isn't going to get me anywhere, is it? All this toing and froing, deliberating and assuming. All will be revealed soon, and I will have them both back with me in no time.' She stood up with renewed vigour and brushed herself down. 'Come on, Trouby, before I start to cry. Let's go and join in all the fun.'

The four o' clock sun was swallowed by a cloud as she poured herself a glass of rose-hip wine. She felt a small bundle of fur brush against her ankles. Thinking it was Troubadour again, she reached down to stroke the top of his head, but when her hand disappeared further than her knees, she held up her skirts and peered down. 'Digger, you got out. Oh, praise the gods, this is a miraculous day.' She looked around. 'Where is your master, girl? Did you run ahead of him?'

The small terrier dropped the scroll at her feet, and without taking her eyes off of her master's intended, started to yap. Her tail was rotating at an excitable speed and her bark had an urgent tone to it.

'Okay, okay, I shall read it,' said Moira, calming her down. 'I hope it brings me good news.' She carefully retrieved the parchment and unraveled it with nimble fingers.

Written in indelible ink on superior quality vellum with the crest of two dragons at the top, the contents were addressed to her.

My dearest Moira,

I hope this letter finds you well, and that everyone escaped unharmed. Everything went according to plan, and I can assure you we won't be bothered by my brother or any of his soldiers again.

Dearest, I must tell you that I am now on my way to see Lace, my daughter. I have been told of her whereabouts and need to speak with her as a matter of urgency. I know you will understand. But please do this one thing for me. In two days' time, I want you to travel west of Aiden Hall to a fortress called Dragons Spire. I am sending out more than a thousand invitations, from the far north of the kingdoms right down to shores of the south. This will be a grand occasion that all will remember. Please bring Troubadour and Digger, they will both have a very important role. My love, in exactly two days' time at 4.00 pm, we shall be wed. Please choose a close friend to help you on the day, and for Philipe to give you away. Then I shall return with you to take up the position that Philipe very kindly offered me.

My love, it won't be long now.
Forever yours,
Coben.

MOIRA READ the parchment over and over again. Tears rolled down her flushed cheeks in droves, she could not curtail her excitement. *What a joyful day this is* she thought. How lucky we all are. Sinking another glass of rose-hip wine, and followed by her two new canine friends, she went to share the news.

AN EVENING of merriment followed with singing, music, dancing, feasting. Some slept peacefully under the stars while others took themselves off to sit by the trees. Philipe sat by Vlavos' grave for a while and thanked his son for everything he had done for him and Saskia, and apologised for everything, that he, as a father, hadn't done. Tiller and Winta sat by the brook, with the gurgle of slow-moving water for company. Dom and Asher leaned against the timbers of the waterwheel, planning their future together at Condor Vale.

And as the crescent moon hung high in a star-studded sky, all thoughts were on the events in two days' time—attending the very grand Dragons Spire.

CHAPTER TWENTY-ONE

The sun was low in the west by the time they came to a halt. The dragon breathed out heavily and Coben felt himself lowered onto a white stallion. A drooping white ostrich plume adorned the headpiece of a silver bridle. He himself wore a richly embroidered crimson cloak atop a grey doublet and grey breeches. Black leather boots cushioned his feet and soft brown gloves felt smooth to the touch. By the time he turned round to thank her again, Sansara had gone.

Coben was still in a trance as he made his way into the clan domain. This was the Marshland Tribe, the furthest north in the Kingdom of Durundal. His daughter had lived here for the last six years. He hadn't seen her since she was ten years old.

A soft green moss grew thickly here, covering fallen stones in great mounds and bearding all the pillars. Vines crept in and out of forgotten windows, through open doors and archways, up the sides of high stone walls and along the grey worn steps. Lichen kissed the exposed exterior, and mould adorned the grand chambers. This was once a place of royalty. A spectacular palace that seated the greatest kings of the land. In its heyday, this palace would have covered several hectares of land, with outbuildings so large they could hold an entire community. The stables could have housed a thousand horses, its granary would have been the size of twenty huts, its four towers once reached up high into the clouds, and its maze of stairs and corridors would have twisted and turned for miles. But the most cavernous room of all was the Great Hall. With its tapestried walls, ornate ceilings, huge hearths, carved oak doors, and pillared surrounds with endless steps up to the royal dais. Nobility from far and wide would come and sit in the Great Hall and partake of the finest wines, succulent pig, and the sweetest vegetables. Sadly, little remained of the splendour and opulence now. The keep lay broken on the riverbed, littered with fragments of the crenelated walls and flying buttresses. All broken. A ruin. A reminder off a distant past, a memory of better times, before greed and avarice was commonplace and death would come in the form of a sword hungry for blood, wrought in hell's furnace, but skilled enough to take an innocent's life.

Clan leader Wargon and his wife Raven had kept it this way. Here, the spirits of the dead merged with the souls of the living, and both kept the memories alive. Wargon had settled here with the sole intention of keeping his clan safe. And he was right. The General and his henchmen had never ventured this far north. No one other than clan had stepped on to this sacred soil, for the stories of troubled apparitions and avenging ghouls travelled far and wide. Widely inaccurate, these exaggerated tales saved the clan. For the Marshland Tribe believed they were gods and kindred spirits who only served to protect them.

A YOUNG MAN APPROACHED HIM. He was tall with wild flaxen hair to his shoulders and wearing the robes of a warrior. His beard was trim, and he stood before Coben granite-strong as if he had been hewn from rock.

'Good evening, sir. Have you travelled far? Maybe you have lost your way. We can take care of your horse and give you food and shelter for the night.'

'Good evening, friend. I am sorry that the hour is so late. And yes, I have travelled a long way and would be glad of some food and shelter for both my horse and I.'

'Certainly, sir. Please, let me take your horse.'

The young man took the reins as Coben jumped down and saw before him a stoic man of strong standing. He pulled the stirrup leathers up stroked the stallion's neck.

'I wonder of you could assist me further, though, young man,' said Coben.

'Of course, sir. How can I help?'

'I am looking for someone and I am told that she lives here.'

The young man looked at his kindly face. Though his dark hooded eyes looked as if they were hiding a thousand tales, most of which he would rather not have witnessed.

'Who is it that you wish to see?'

'I am looking for Lace.'

The young man looked startled.

'And whom shall I say is asking for her?'

'I am Coben, her father.'

The younger man peered at the visitor closely. He could actually see a vague resemblance. This was truly remarkable, and he longed to hear more of his story. He extended an arm in a warm handshake.

'I am so pleased to meet you, sir. My name is Torré, and I am married to your daughter.'

'She is married? You are her husband?' asked Coben returning the gesture.

'She is and I am.'

Coben then ran his hand through his few remaining strands of hair. 'Goodness me, I last saw her when she was ten years old. And now she is married.'

'She is, sir.'

'Do you have any children?'

'Not yet,' Torré laughed. 'There have been a few battles to take care of recently. We have had little time.'

Coben nodded knowingly.

'But it won't be long now, I can promise you that.'

Coben gripped the man and pulled him into an embrace. 'Thank you for taking care of her, young man. I can see you have the strength of a lion, and I am already very proud of you.'

'You wait till you see your daughter, then, kind sir. She has the heart of a pride of lions and more.'

Coben slapped him on the back and followed Torré to a stable block where a stable hand took charge of the horse, then he followed Torré further into the camp.

Lace was sitting outside, teasing a reluctant fire to flame. Her long golden hair hung loose to her narrow waist, and a few braids at the front were pinned up to her crown. She looked up and smiled as Torré came back into view.

'Lace, I have someone here to see you.'

Without a word, she looked at the visitor and tilted her head, then she narrowed her eyes.'

In the firelight, Coben could see her steel blue eyes were just like her mother's—so pale and pure that the pupils shone out like solid pieces of jet. He stepped forward into the light. 'Do you recognise me now?'

'Father, is that you?' She was tentative at first. She could hardly remember a life with him, it had been so long. But gradually, the more she looked at him, the memories came flooding back. As she unravelled her tall, lean frame, she fell into his open arms, wreathing her own around his sturdy neck.

'How did you find me, Father? How did you know I was here?'

'There is much to tell and I will share all of it with you later, but for now, I want to sit and look at you, for you have grown into a fine young woman.'

Lace smiled. 'You must be hungry, Father. Have you come a long way?'

'All in good time, Lace. All in good time.'

Lace asked Torré to fetch a platter of food for them all. 'This is going to be a long night, and I feel we will all need some refreshments.' She sat back down and motioned for her father to join her.

'I have missed you so much, Lace, I have never stopped thinking about you.'

'You have always been in my thoughts, Father. Always.'

'Things have happened that have made me question my life. Why did I go? Why didn't I stay?' His heart was heavy.

'Father, you were trying to provide for us. I know that. Mother knew that also.'

He stopped her. He was shaking his head. 'Lace, I must ease this awful burden from my mind this very evening before I share anything else with you.'

'Of course, Father. What vexes you so?'

'I know that something terrible happened to you when you were much younger, something that could have been avoided if I were with you.' He closed his stinging eyes and held her hands in his own. 'I went to sea as a merchant seaman to make my fortune, as you know. And yes, I wanted to provide for my family. But when I returned and saw that my homestead was gone, I changed into a man I did not recognise.' He paused as he composed himself. 'I went to work for my brother, and under his orders, I have witnessed far too much death. I have seen families torn apart and communities ravaged.' He hung his head low as he remembered. 'But I hope you believe me when I say I am not part of that world anymore. I do not fight. I do not want bloodshed. I can't call myself a father unless I relinquish the past, and I know I have done that now. I have been given another chance.'

He leaned forward and kissed her cheek.

She squeezed his hand in return. 'Father, we live in a changing world. I, too, have seen terrible things. Things that a young girl should never see. But I have grown, and I have changed as well.'

He smiled at her maturity, her humility, and her courage. He could see what Torré meant when he said she had the heart of a pride of lions. He knew she was strong enough to recall those dreadful days. He knew that they could talk about it now.

'Lace, can you tell me what happened all those years ago?'

Torré returned with some food and ale and pulled up a chair. Coben took a flagon and swigged it down in one go.

Lace stared at the moonlight as it streamed across the sky. Her father had returned to her. She was complete now. All those long-forgotten memories came surging back again. She let out a long sigh through her nose and held on to him tightly, then she closed her eyes for a moment and went back to the time when she was fourteen years old.

'THEY CAME AT DAWN. The rumble rolled over the hills like thunder, the dust spiralled into plumes of billowing clouds that fed into the chaos. We knew it wasn't thunder then. We knew it was something even more deadly that would rip our community apart. We could hear the sound of weapons grating against the thunder of hooves—spears, sickles, axes—all ready to chop and swing. Our beating hearts pulsed heavy with anticipation and wide eyes fixed on the deadly horizon. A flaming arrow curled into the night sky, and arrows curved down from the hillside, sending fire balls of oil-soaked liniment into our fragile homes. The impact was brutal as an orange ball of flame exploded across the courtyard scattering the splintered frames of wooden enclosures.

'The community was ablaze and continued to burn as more arrows were fired. Like streams of lava from an erupting volcano, the men came into our peaceful little community, and none of us knew why.

'Arrows flew their course and plunged into the chaos of shrieking people and stricken animals. Women running for cover were trampled by the invading hoards. Children were crying in their mother's arms. Our men were trying to control the fire, and others screamed in agony as they became engulfed in flames. Mother ran to the forest with me, and we could only watch in fear at the dreadful slaughter before our eyes.'

Coben bit down on his knuckles.

'There was nothing we could do, just try and stay silent and invisible until it was all over. Ruben was crying — he was only ten years old and terrified. Mother was white with fear but trying to ease our panic. *"It will soon be over,"* she said, trying to curtail her own terror. *"The soldiers will get what they came for and then they will be gone."*

'But they didn't go. They enjoyed the sport, enjoyed terrifying the women and children, the elderly and the other innocents.' Lace shook her head as the memories came flooding back. 'So futile, so pointless ... so cowardly.' Her voice was gravely.

'The flashing lights of fire and the constant stream of wailing terrified us. The carnage was still going on in front of us. We covered our ears to block out the screams. Ruben had his eyes shut the whole time. The soldiers were finding people and lining them up—men, women and children. I saw my grandmother and grandfather herded like animals to the pitiful line. It seemed the only way to survive the attack was to not fight back. Too many had already lost their lives by doing so.' Deep in reverie, she took a few more steadying breaths and closed her eyes before she continued. 'Still the screams raged, and the whinny of petrified horses echoed in the valley. It was our very worst nightmare.

'And then we heard it. The General had found us. He hoisted me up in front of him and marched my mother and brother to the line of captives. Mother collapsed into her parents. On reflection, that was the worst thing she could do, because now the General knew they were related.'

'To their cost,' said Torré with a grim retort.

'We were all now prisoners of the General, and I was to be his plaything.'

'Did he hurt you? Did he... touch you?' Coben could barely say the words.

'No, Father, he didn't.'

'What then?'

'He wanted to dance with me.'

'What?' Coben couldn't believe what he had just

heard.

'That's what my maid told me when I arrived. *"That's all he wants you for. He might smell you and taste your feminine sweat, but he won't hurt you. His kingdom is so brutal as it is. He just likes to dance with a beautiful girl."*

'I remember it well. The third night I was there, he gave me a luxurious gown to wear with soft doe-skin slippers to put on my feet. He pulled me downstairs into the ballroom from where the most beautiful music was coming from. I remember stopping in my tracks as all manner of birds flew in and out of the open doors to the tune of the harmonies—pink flamingos, white doves, blue peacocks, turquoise kingfishers, yellow canaries, green parrots—there were so many exquisite varieties. I couldn't believe such beauty existed.'

Lace smiled at the memory. But it was short lived as the reason for her captivity was revealed.

'He ordered me to dance. The look on my face was enough to anger him. *"Don't just stand there gawping girl. Come here!"* He pulled me close and began to move around in time to the music. This soldier, this tyrant, this destroyer of lives liked to dance. It was all too surreal.'

Coben sat back in his chair. He hadn't even noticed Torré take hold of her hand. Lace leaned into him. Even the great Torré hadn't heard the extent of what his wife had been through.

'How did you escape?' Coben was ashen and his voice weak.

'I had a guard and a maid. Neither were very vigilant, and I was able to walk around at my leisure. I remember going for a walk. I could see the boys—our boys—being taught to fight with weapons they had never seen before, let alone used. I saw the vast arena and was petrified for them.' She wiped away a tear. 'It was an instinctive reaction. I just saw an opportunity, and I took it. One minute I was in the palace, and the next I was in the back of a goods wagon.'

'A goods wagon?'

'Yes, I had seen it many times arrive at the palace. It seemed like the perfect escape. To tuck myself away and get through the gates unnoticed.'

'Where were you going, though?'

'I wanted to get help. To get our boys and my family out of there.'

Coben shook his head, angry that he was not there to protect his family, and bitter that he did not kill the General and the Emperor himself.

'When the wagon stopped, I peered through the crease of the blanket. We had stopped at the harbour. It was teaming with people. People who could help. I jumped out of the wagon and ran up to them, grabbing them, urging them to help me, telling them what I had seen. But they looked at me as though I was mad and recoiled in my presence. Some threw things. Most ignored me. All were terrified of this lunatic child who by now was grubby, frantic and disheveled. A group of boys chased me for a long way. It was fun to them. To me, I had gone from one nightmare to another. I ran as fast as I could with no idea of where I was going. But then I found a rowing boat moored against some railings. I had barely enough time to look around, untie the rope, and jump inside. I flattened myself on the base and let the boat take me up the river. I lay in there for days—too scared to get out. I didn't want the angry mob to find me. I just let the boat take me as far away as possible.

'One day, it grounded itself on the bend of an inlet. By now I was very weak and hungry, so I had to get out. Here, though, I could see new shoots. The bulbs were big and juicy with clovers, dandelions, wood-sorrel, and purslane. I followed a path and kept walking and walking and walking. Through the rain and through the fog. When the sun beat down so hard my back would burn, still I walked. I ate wolf spiders with their egg sacs still attached, and slow moving grubs, and resting insects. I ate everything that I could find in the forest—I was that hungry. I found burrows in the ground and hollows in trees where I would curl up and rest. And that's when Torré found me—a very young girl, exhausted, alone and frightened who by now had lost her way and her family.'

Loving eyes fell on her husband, and she reached for his hand. Coben smiled at the open affection.

'How did you find out about your mother?'

'When I relayed the story back to Wargon and Raven, they told me that my mother, brother, and grandparents couldn't be found. It was only several years later that Wargon told me the truth... that the General had put them into a wagon and set fire to it. They were burnt alive. It was a stark warning to others, and a punishment for me.'

Torré moved closer and put a comforting arm around her. Coben looked to the ground, blotting the tears with the back of his hand.

'All the clans for miles around had been told of this

barbaric monster and how he rounded up clan boys for his games. This is how Wargon discovered the fate of my family. Our clan had been the first in his sickening games and that's why our home was attacked: to steal our lads for entertainment. Word soon got round, though.' She looked up to the sky and breathed heavily through her nose. 'Other clans were more prepared than us, but none of them could stop the wrath of the General.'

'I came looking for you,' Coben started. 'When I docked in port I went to the homestead and found nothing but charred bones and a graveyard of memories. A farmer passing by told me what had happened there and where you had all gone. When I got to Ataxata, it was too late. The games had been and gone and my family had been slain. Though I was told that you had escaped. And from that day on, I have prayed that you were safe and had found a new home.'

'I did. I was lucky. Torré has looked after me since the day he found me. He taught me how to hunt, how to fight, and how to be the very best with a bow and arrow.'

Coben smiled. 'I know another young lady who sounds just like you. She changed me. She was instrumental in my transformation. I will tell you all about Saskia and her fascination with moths later.'

Lace smiled affectionately. 'I look forward to hearing about her. And speaking of moths, look at this.' She turned around and showed her father a female emperor moth which covered the whole of her back. Painted in blue and purple, red and grey, the top wings spread across each shoulder blade, and the bottom wings curved round her lower back. Four large black vacuoles sat on each wing that signified her rear eyes. The body of the saturniid ran down her spine, and the antenna reached towards her shoulders.

'The moth. You have always been fascinated with moths.' He gasped in awe.

'I have father, but this tattoo represents far more than my fascination. This represents my metamorphosis from a young, frightened little girl to a warrior who can fight back. From the moment I crawled out of that blanket, I became a fighter. And I don't take any prisoners now. I cheered when Skyrah put her dagger through the General's heart, and I punched the air when I discovered she had killed the Emperor. She is my hero, my kindred spirit, and I am forever in her debt.'

'We all are,' said Torré stoically. 'And Namir and Lyall, they are the true heroes of our generation.'

'Hear, hear,' said Lace, leaning into him again. 'But come, Father, enough about me. I want to hear all about you. And after we have eaten, you must tell me of your travels, where you have been all this time, and how you came to find me.'

Coben was hungry enough to eat anything right now, but after the first few bites, he slowed down to appreciate the taste. The fish had been roasted to perfection, and the boiled vegetables were crisp and at the right stage of tenderness. Then the wild strawberries that followed had him murmuring with pleasure. His mouth watered with each sweet bite, for he hadn't tasted food this good for eons, it seemed.

It pleased Lace immensely that he enjoyed his food. She watched as Coben nodded in satisfaction and she put a large leg of chicken on his plate before he started to relay his story.

'Whatever you hear now, you must believe. These are not the rantings of a delusional old man. I will tell you things that seem impossible, highly improbable. But remember that we live in a world where everything is decided by what we can see and what we touch. If we can't see it or we don't understand it, then we perceive that it doesn't exist. But it does exist, and what may seem impossible here, is in fact highly probable in another world.'

CHAPTER TWENTY-TWO

Sansara called to her dragon. The blue-green vision swept down beside her. The blue stone lit up against her chest, and as it grew to the size of her fist, the indigo cleared and a spectacle unfolded.

A STAG STOOD in the shadows, eating fruits, acorns and nuts from the ground. The great beast was unsuspecting, and his rack of antlers weighed heavily on his crown. The sun pierced through the thorns and lit up the harvest for him. He glanced up occasionally to survey his domain, his mouth rotating with the succulent vegetation.

'Shh, don't make a sound.'

Dainn drew an arrow from its quiver and placed it in the bow. One shot was all it would take. He aimed and drew back carefully on the string....

But the stag suddenly moved, alerted by a movement behind him. It veered quickly out of sight, but Dainn's arrow had already been released and found the heart of the man who had alerted the beast.

Cornelius dropped to the ground. Saskia screamed his name. A flock of birds took flight, the dust was still settling from the stag's departure.

Ajeya ran up to them and held her hands to her mouth.

Saskia was holding onto him, her hands covered in blood.

'What happened?'

'This is your brother,' Saskia managed to whisper.

'No, it cannot be. I was told he is dead.'

'He survived the stabbing and the fall.'

'Only a stag in the shadows can kill me.' His voice struggled.

Saskia remembered the conversation and sobbed into his chest. 'But the stag didn't kill you, my love.'

Ajeya was visibly shocked, hardly believing what was happening. She dropped to her knees and took hold of his hand. He looked up at her and saw the thin pale line carved into her face. He shivered. He remembered. He felt the stab of remorse. He saw a figure leaning over the crib. A monster. He choked back the memory from when he was only three.

'Beware a stag in the shadows, for he has the power to slay you.'

'What's he saying?' Ajeya looked at Saskia.

'He made a pact for immortality. That's how he survived the stabbing and the fall. But a stag in the shadows can slay him.'

Ajeya looked at Saskia again, the whites of her eyes

frantic. Her voice was tremulous. 'Dainn has the totem of a stag.'

Saskia looked up at Dainn.

'I'm so sorry.' His voice was weak. 'I didn't see him.'

'It was an accident.' she said. 'You didn't know.'

'What can we do?' Ajeya managed to say. 'We can't let him die. I've already lost one brother. I can't lose another one before I've gotten to know him.'

'I lost my brother, too, Ajeya, and Cornelius has helped me live again. I can't lose him, either. I just can't.'

Cornelius winced with the pain.

'Help him, please. Someone help him.' Ajeya's wails echoed into the forest.

Cornelius opened his eyes. He was warm now, and the light was golden. He was covered in a white sheet. He felt unusually calm. He must be *dead* now. This was *death*. The last time he thought he was dead, he was feeling cold and covered in a blanket of snow. That time it was grey like his skin. This time it was different. He peeled back the sheet and looked at his torso—there was no injury. He looked at his hands—they were heathy and even skin-toned. He felt his face—it was smooth and young. He saw Saskia crying. He felt his sister stroking his face. It was then that he screamed out loud.

'No, not now, please not now. I have just found love. I have been reunited with my sister. My mother is waiting for me. My enemies are no more.'

He heard a voice in his head.

'Your daughter can save you.'

'My daughter. Yes. Please. Let her save me.'

'You will lose your immortality.'

'I don't care. I want to marry Saskia and be a good husband. I want to be a brother to Ajeya and make amends. I want to see my mother again and say sorry.'

'Are you ready to meet your daughter? To be the father she needs in your mortal world?'

'I am ready. I will protect her. I will take care of her. I will love her. I will be a good father to her.'

'Call her then, Cornelius. Call your daughter. Call her name out loud, then she will come.'

'SANSARA!!

CHAPTER TWENTY-THREE

The orb was still rotating and spinning, breathing golds and reds to keep it alive. The great sphere would not settle until it had divulged all the secrets the Fates had commanded. Sansara looked further back still, watching her father's life unravel before her.

Cornelius had been born twenty-five years ago, the only son and heir to the Empress Eujena and Emperor Gnaeus. By the time he was five years old, his mother had gone. It was said that she had given birth to a deformed daughter, not of this world, and certainly not sired by the Emperor. Whatever the truth was, Eujena had been banished from the court, and Cornelius grew up without his mother or a sibling.

By the time he was twelve years old, he was a tall, strong boy with a taste for music, poetry and the arts. He loved singing and had a wonderful voice. So many times, the palace was alive with the sounds of his warbling, and the corridors and galleries rang out daily with his harmonious melodies. This disappointed the Emperor who had wanted a boy who enjoyed hunting, sword fighting, and horsemanship—all the things he wanted to share with his only son. The Emperor had little time for *women's stuff*, as he called it. As the Emperor lost interest in Cornelius, people were brought in to try and change him. No one succeeded.

The Marquis de Beauchamp was one such man, and although he was skilled in hunting, sword fighting, and horsemanship, he appreciated the gentle side of Master Cornelius. He was more sympathetic and understanding, so he encouraged his softer side and formed a strong bond with the boy.

The Marquis was a few years older than Cornelius though some said they looked about the same age. Cornelius had been given a privileged life, whilst the Marquis had covered his well. He was slight of shoulder, not overly tall, but a medium build with a kind face and sparkling eyes. The Marquis kept his head shaved and wore a tattoo on his left arm: a Smilodon, the emblem of his tribe and a reminder of his forefathers from whence he had come. Though no one ever knew from whence he had come. No one knew his roots or how he had learned his craft, only that he was skilled in many things.

After answering a notice to be an aide for Master Cornelius at the palace, he had been assessed by Domitrius Corbulo by way of a sword fight with his best swordsman. In addition, he was made to trap a boar in the forest, and skin a rabbit in less than twenty seconds. He was given the position immediately. Cornelius liked him because he was always smiling. He had a soft kind voice and he always had an answer to everything Cornelius asked him.

'Where do dragons and witches come from?'

'On the other side of the world, Master Cornelius. That's where they come from. They can't hurt you because they are so far away. Strange people live on the other side of the world, and that's why no one goes there, only deviants and non-human souls.'

'I won't be going there, then.'

'Of course, you won't. You are a kind and gentle boy and have no place with those kinds of people.'

BY THE TIME Cornelius was fourteen years old, his father was obsessed with even more power and driven by avarice. He was fearful of his dynasty and how Cornelius would fare in matters of war. Would he even be able to father a worthy son, or would he just breed more weaklings like his firstborne?

'How come I am cursed with a fool for a son? How will he sit on the throne and rule when I have gone?'

'Maybe he should come with us when we search for the Seal of Kings, Your Excellency,' Domitrius Corbulo had suggested. 'That way he will have to face death. It will definitely toughen him up—it's the only way to make him a man.'

'Excellent idea, Corbulo.' The Emperor had agreed jubilantly.

But all that happened was the General and the Captains put Cornelius in perilous situations, and he always came off worse for wear. He got knocked down by more experienced men, and he vomited when he saw death. He was put on the most difficult stallions that he couldn't control. Every day, there was something more challenging that Master Cornelius couldn't handle. And every time, General Domitrius Corbulo and his captains sat laughing while he struggled.

The Marquis had observed all of this and went to the Emperor many times. 'My lord, if I may be so bold. I am concerned that Master Cornelius is being subjected to a form of bullying and expected to do things that he is not yet proficient in.'

'Beauchamp!' The Emperor turned purple with rage. 'When I want your advice, I will ask for it. When I want a lecture on how to bring up my son, I will ask for it. When I want to know the musical arrangement of a string quartet, I will ask for it. As I haven't asked for any of those things, will you leave me to do as I see fit?'

'But, my lord, Master Cornelius offers other gifts that are far superior to killing and fighting.'

The Marquis was kicked out of the room with the Emperor's wrath still ringing in his ears.

By the time the boy was eighteen years old, the Emperor had witnessed enough, and of course, Corbulo was there with the solution.

'He will never be fit to be an Emperor like yourself, Gnaeus. He is weak with too much of his mother in him. He is a laughingstock and dishonours you.'

'So, what am I to do with him, Corbulo?'

'I have heard of places where boys such as him are sent away to become men.'

The Emperor was now interested and leaned in to allow Corbulo free passage.

'I can sort this out for you, Gnaeus. I can send him to the other side of the world where he has to face his fears and become a man. It is not a nice place, I can assure you, but then again, the world in which we live is not that nice.'

'Do it,' said the Emperor gleefully.

Cornelius was beside himself with grief and pleaded with his father to change his mind. 'Please, Father, please do not send me away, I will try harder, I promise. I will fight. I will charge a horse with the General. I will hunt and kill with the Marquis. I will do anything you ask—just don't send me away.'

The Marquis had also pleaded to no avail. 'Your Grace, you cannot send him away. Why do you want to change him? He has so much more to offer than fighting and killing and jousting on a horse. He is a kind and gentle boy who believes that dragons and witches live on the other side of the world. You cannot do it to him. He is your son. He is your flesh and blood.'

'How dare you speak to me like this? Who do you think you are? I had a wife once who begged me to let her stay here with another mutant of a child that was supposedly mine. And guess what I said to her?'

The Marquis suddenly lost the sparkle in his eyes when he looked at the madman in front of him. 'No, of course dragons and witches don't exist. There are far worse things to contend with.'

The Emperor continued. 'And you had better tell

that pathetic excuse of a boy soon, because the arrangements are being made as we speak.'

'Please, Your Grace. He is your son, and you do not know what it is like to be out there on your own with no one to look out for you.'

'Ha,' cried the Emperor with indignation. 'As I have already told you, I exiled my wife and her hideous excuse of a daughter to the great wilderness on their own, so I have no hesitation at all in doing the same to her son.' He paused to draw breath without a flicker of remorse. 'I am tiring of you and your ramblings. You forget your place in this palace. I should have you locked up in the deepest dungeon and throw away the key for speaking to me the way you do. But as you are so irritatingly concerned about my son's welfare, perhaps you should go with him. Then I won't have to set eyes on either of you again.'

Beauchamp clenched his teeth. 'I will go with him... gladly. I will look out for him... happily. I will never leave his side. You can count on that.' He bowed his way out of the room.

SANSARA SAW IT ALL. She had witnessed her father's demise from a sweet natured boy to a tyrant. But there was still one more thing to view. The reason the Fates had brought her here and what she was required to do. The orb took her further back... to when Cornelius was just three years old. It was a few days after the birth of his sister, and a sinister turn of events changed the shape of the future. She shuddered as the events unravelled before her. She could not believe what she had just witnessed.

The orb was still spinning and rotating, there was more to see, and she watched as a younger Ajeya and Dainn sat side by side in a cave. Their innocence endearing, their love for each other immense. Sansara felt a tug at her heart as she remembered her own longing for another. But it was brief and short lived. The orb pulled her into its core.

'What happened to your face?' Dainn asked her.

She nearly choked on her tea. 'Where did that come from?'

'I am sorry. I didn't mean to embarrass you.' His voice was sincere.

'You haven't embarrassed me, you just took me by surprise.'

He couldn't resist, and he reached to feel the contours of her cheek. His touch held her motionless. She couldn't pull away. She felt his fingers as they traced the imperfection and watched as his eyes followed the thin pale line. He wasn't even aware of her breathing quicken as she tingled with the touch. He just thought of her as a beautiful woman with an incredible strength at her core. And yet this disfigurement made her vulnerable and fragile, like a butterfly with a creased wing; and he knew that he would love her forever.

'You are an amazing woman, Ajeya, and so very special. Not only do you have a beautiful face, but you are so strong and determined. You have a good heart, you are an exemplary horse woman, and without doubt, a most formidable warrior.'

She blushed. 'Thank you.' She felt her face and touched it delicately. 'I was born like this... and have faced my fair share of prejudice to be sure; but instead of disempowering me, it has defined me and made me stronger.'

He smiled at her humility and traced the line with a keen eye. 'It looks more of a knife wound to me.'

Her fingers reached up as if to feel it for the first time. 'No... it cannot be. Who would have done such a thing to a newborn baby? Besides, my mother would have known. No... it became visible when I was two days old. It's just one of those unexplainable things that I've had to live with.'

He raised an eyebrow, incredulous, but brushed the concern from her face and kissed the imperfection. She felt warm and safe next to him. With his statuesque height and broad shoulders and body covered in a soft golden down, he really was like a god, and any deformity at birth had healed long ago. Nevertheless, she still found herself asking the question. 'So, what happened to your legs?'

He stretched them out before him and tensed up the powerful muscles. 'I was born with twisted legs, though you wouldn't know it now. My mother and father insisted on fitting splints and did lots of muscle building exercises, so now I am strong and the same as any other man.'

'You are more than any other man,' she said with acumen. 'You have an extraordinary strength and an empowering way about you. The way you see things, the way you feel things. It makes me wonder if people like us are given another sense, a special ability from a greater force to make up for our affliction.'

'Maybe we do,' he said thoughtfully. 'But maybe we just appreciate everything we have overcome, and therefore see things in a different way.'

'Yes, maybe you are right.'

'We are both right—because we are both survivors.'

Sansara felt the warm tear run down her face. Was it for her own lost love or was it because she had witnessed the innocence between these two young people? But even more significant was how Dainn had questioned the validity of Ajeya's story.

A conversation played out in the sphere. It must be important, she thought. Her tears dried instantly. It was Eujena, the mother and Ariane, the child's maid.

'Will they accept my child?' Eujena's voice quivered.

Ariane nodded. 'You have no choice, my lady. But Ajeya must never know the truth. You must never reveal to her what we know to be true.'

Eujena dipped her head in despair and nodded.

'To everyone who meets her, she was born like it. She must never know. No one must know.'

Eujena nodded again. 'She will never know from me.'

The orb stopped. It returned to the size of her thumb and a static colour of indigo concealed the magic. All would be revealed soon, she thought to herself. There would be no more burning questions after tonight.

. . .

'Where weaves the path, oh mystic Fates? Of magic and spells from life first breath to the key of death's gates. And betwixt and between, life's shadows hide in enchanted ground. Thou wanderer, thou spirit, the Fates await. Your secret has been found.'

CHAPTER TWENTY-FOUR

THE DRAGON CURLED its tail round to lift her onto its nape. She leaned forward and took hold of the horns. The staff was secured firmly at her side.

'Take me to Cornelius.'

The instruction was obeyed, and the dragon launched into the sky and followed the course of the river back down to the Clan of the Giant's Claw.

THE SUMMER AIR WAS COOL, and tiny fireflies drifted and shimmered in the diminishing sunlight, so it seemed they were journeying through an enchanted vortex. It was as though the air sensed danger around them, and the trees and hedgerows quivered constantly beneath the bulk of the dragon.

The flight was short. Sansara sensed they were nearing the end of their journey as a vast canyon appeared before them, and the might of the dragon's leathery wings began to slow. The mountains that bordered each side of the valley sloped into a ripple of hills, and the river looked like ribbons of silver, winding its way through the pass. Here, the route exposed a wide expanse of land where forest and glades turned the landscape green, and below she saw a group of people hunched over a figure. She recognised them at once, and as the shadow of her dragon turned it dark for several minutes, she prepared to make her descent.

She heard Cornelius calling for her.

'Sansara, help me. Please help me.'

The three people around him stood back in alarm as she made her entrance. The orb was pulsating on her chest, the staff burning like a white-hot flame.

'Please do not fear me. I am Sansara, his daughter, born from his mortal seed and the fire of my mother's womb.'

'He told me about you,' said Saskia, feeling her mouth anxiously drying. 'He told me how his daughter would bring salvation and peace to the lands.'

Sansara smiled. 'Indeed, that is one of my tasks, but my main task on this mission is to save my father.'

Saskia knelt before the sorceress, her head bowed low between her hands. Ajeya bent one knee and placed her hand on her heart. Dainn unsheathed his sword, and kneeling before the goddess, plunged the tip into the ground and learned his head against the hilt.

Sansara stood over Cornelius and ran the staff over his body. It glowed brightly in her hands. A white light made the others shield their eyes, their vision suspended as the magic began to work. They heard enchanted words as if from another tongue. These words were repeated, and the commands grew louder. The ground beneath them trembled and the trees around them shook. A wind picked up pace and the long fingers of dust caressed their frozen faces. Meanwhile, all the time, Sansara was delivering her empowering orders. Small tornados whipped the ground, and through slits of tightly-closed eyes, they could see something moving. Cornelius was being lifted higher and higher. The staff was underneath him and held him suspended in the air. Still, Sansara rang out her commands in tongues of the sorceress.

The wind grew brutal. The tornadoes aggravated. Sansara raised her pitch a decibel higher. The light went out from the sky. The dark clung to them like a shroud. Three heartbeats could be heard in the maelstrom. Louder and louder, the beats drummed. Then they detected a fourth. The wind subsided. The tornadoes ceased. The pitch black gave way to the sun. The beating hearts softened.

Now they could open their eyes.

They watched in awe as Cornelius made his descent to the ground and stood before them looking regal and handsome with not a wound on his body. He looked down at his apparel and felt for evidence of injury. There was none. He spun around as if seeing light for the first time. His eyes squinted, and his brow furrowed. He reached for Sansara's hand and instantly noticed that the **H** had gone from his wrist. And as he scoured the limb for scars, a new apparel replaced his worn-out robes.

Now he bore a doublet of dark blue silk edged in satin. Across his chest. an engrailed dragon had been embroidered in gold thread. His breeches were the finest white cotton, and on his feet were the softest leather shoes.

'Am I alive or dead?'

'You are alive, Father.'

He pulled Sansara into his embrace and kissed her face.

'My dearest daughter, I cannot thank you enough. I cannot believe what has happened to me these past few days. And now I see how lucky I am, and none more so than to have fathered such an exquisite beauty.'

She leaned into him. 'I know what has happened over these past few days. I have been privy to much information. I have also seen much of your life, in fact, from your very first days. So, I feel I have known you forever.'

'How bizarre is that concept.' He smiled.' It should be the other way round.'

She pushed a laugh through her nose. Here. Look into the orb, and you will see my life.'

The orb grew in her hands and the constellation started swirling and bringing its contents to life. He saw everything—from her birth, to her first steps, to her first words—and her life on Mawi Island before she was given this task.

'It seems impossible that this has happened to me.' His words chased the shadows of confusion.

'When you question the validity of the impossible, that's when you question hope.' Her words were profound.

'Just believe what I see, and don't question what I hear?'

'In matters like this, yes.'

He felt Saskia's hand on his shoulder, and he reached round for it.

'This is my Saskia. My wife to be.' He kissed her hand softly and looked deep into her eyes.

'Yes, I know who Saskia is.' Sansara smiled at the introduction.

'And this is my sister, and her husband Dainn.'

'Ajeya, yes, I know who you are. And Dainn, I have watched you as well.' Sansara stroked the scar on Ajeya's face. It took her back to her dream.

THE ROOM WAS MUSTY, *and a small beam of light fell on a richly-decorated granite tomb. On the top, a man and a woman lay next to each other. They both held swords to their breasts, and they both wore crowns. She noticed the relief of a hare and a stag on the side of the coffin alongside some names that she couldn't decipher. Sansara trembled as she ran a finger across the woman's smooth porcelain face. She imagined she saw her take a sharp intake of breath when she felt a line carved into her cheek. Sansara recoiled instantly and her gaze fell on the man at her side. A trickle of red blood ran from an arrow wound in his heart.*

NOW SHE UNDERSTOOD IT. Now she could embrace it

and learn from it. She blew lightly on the line carved into Ajeya's cheek, and instantly it disappeared.

'You won't be needing that anymore, Ajeya. It has defined you as a person and carved you into a warrior. But its purpose has been served. I relinquish you of the mark.'

Ajeya reached up to feel her smooth, porcelain skin. There was no indentation, no pull of the skin, no tug at the eye. A warm tear ran down her face. Dainn turned to hold her tight. They were both lost in the emotion and Cornelius stepped forward. There was concern in his eyes, and a trembling in his tone. But the pull to divulge all over-ran every other emotion.

'I have something to tell you, Ajeya. I have held onto this awful secret for over twenty years. And now I have to release this heavy burden that I have carried since I was a small boy of three.'

Ajeya wiped the tip of her nose with a finger. Dainn spun round, a crinkled frown emerging. The need to hear what he knew to be true was consuming.

Ajeya began to slowly shake her head.

'Please, brother, no. Please tell me it's not true.' She gripped Dainn's hand tightly, remembering what he had said to her on so many occasions.

Cornelius nodded his head and hung it in shame. 'It's true... and—'

'Stop!' The sorceress stepped forward.

'Ajeya needs to know. She needs to know the truth. She needs to hear it from me.' He was adamant.

'And she will, Father. She will know the truth. Today. Right here. Right now.

'But she needs to hear it from me. I have to tell her that it was—' His voice was muted. The wand had rendered him speechless.

Instead, he watched the orb grow bigger and brighter, and all the constellations from the past twenty-two years brought those dreadful events back to life again.

CHAPTER TWENTY-FIVE

'It's a girl. It's a beautiful baby girl.' The nurse fussed over the new baby and gave her to Eujena for suckling.

'She is so beautiful,' gushed Eujena, 'And look at her perfect skin.' She stroked the little round cheek with the back of a crooked finger.

'She is that, my lady. Complete with ten little fingers and ten little toes.'

Eujena laughed. 'I think the Emperor should come and see his daughter, and Master Cornelius should see his new sister. They have both been so excited.'

'Of course, my lady. I shall tell them that you are both well and are excited to show off the new heiress.'

Eujena hummed to her baby who slept peacefully in her arms. Then she stroked her perfect cheeks and looked at the pink little fingers again and checked the toes. 'You are so perfect. So beautiful.' She kissed the downy head and looked up at the knock at the door.

'Come in, come in.' She called out.

The Emperor and their son rushed in. Three-year-old Cornelius leaned in to see the baby.

'Can I play with her?' he asked. 'I have brought her one of my toys.'

The Emperor laughed. 'She's too young to play with your toys, my boy. She just needs milk and lots of cuddles right now.'

Eujena smiled at her husband and put a hand out to stroke her son's golden hair. 'Your father is right, Cornelius. 'All this little baby needs is lots of love. And I know that you can give her that.'

Cornelius nodded his head 'She can have my picture, though, can't she?'

'Of course, she can. What have you drawn?'

The Emperor smiled as he handed the creased parchment to Eujena. At first, she saw the word ajeya under what looked like the drawing of a hare. But when Cornelius turned it the right way round for her. It actually said the words *a hare* over his drawing of a blue moon.

'This is very clever, Cornelius. Did you do this all by yourself?'

He looked at the nurse who was still tidying things away. 'Well, I had a little bit of help. Nurse said it's a blue moon, and you can see a hare in a blue moon. So, she helped me draw it.'

Eujena saw her wink at Cornelius and smiled.

'Well I think I have just chosen her name, because I like the way your picture changes. This is little Ajeya, everyone. Our very own little hare.'

The nurse nodded in silent agreement, Cornelius

beamed with pride, and Gnaeus hooked a finger over the downy blanket to get more of a peep.

'I think we should let the Emperor hold his new daughter, don't you?'

Cornelius nodded.

The smile spread across her face as she handed the warm bundle to the father.

'She certainly is a beauty,' said the Emperor. 'She has your nose but definitely has my eyes.'

'And she is fair like you...' Eujena's sleepy voice trailed off.

The Emperor looked at her lovingly. 'I think Mama needs some rest now, Cornelius. She is very tired. We shall take your baby sister to her room and show her the new crib.'

'And I can put my picture on her nursery wall.'

'Of course, you can, son. It's a fine picture.'

Gnaeus curved a half smile to Eujena and led his two children into the hallway.

Cornelius took his father's hand and skipped all the way to the nursery. There, he positioned his drawing on the chest of drawers and then moved his new sturdy stool over to the crib.

AS THE DAYS ROLLED BY, Cornelius became even more protective of his new sibling and spent as much time with her as he could. A wooden stool was always positioned so he could peer into the cot and hold her hands, touch her face, or leave another toy. He sat drawing pictures when his mother fed her and stood by when the Nurse tended to her duties.

His parents stood at the door one day and watched him fussing over his sister.

'Look how proud he is, Gnaeus,' said Eujena, leaning into her husband.

'I know. He is going to be a wonderful big brother.' Gnaeus kissed his wife on the top of her head and held her close. 'We are so fortunate, Eujena, and me most of all, because I have the most beautiful wife and the most perfect children.'

Cornelius smiled at them both and held his sister's hand. Eujena softy planted a kiss on her husband's cheek.

'Come now, Cornelius. It's time for bed. Let me read you story, and we can leave Ajeya to sleep.' His mother allowed him a few more minutes and then gently led him back to his room.

The Emperor stood at the cradle for the longest time. The baby lay on her back, her arms above her head and a soft pink blanket rippled at her feet. He watched the gentle rise and fall of her chest and her chin pucker as she slept. She let out little moans and a worried frown creased her brow. The Emperor couldn't pull himself away—he wanted to stand guard and watch her dream. A tear plopped to the floor. He wiped the next one away. 'I am your father, dearest Ajeya. I will always love you and take care of you. I have a duty to rule my kingdom, but my responsibility is to protect you. Sleep tight, little Ajeya. The angels will stand at your helm every night. There will always be someone watching over you. I promise.'

He gently blew out the candle and tip-toed out of the room.

THAT SAME NIGHT, Cornelius was woken by a bad dream. He tossed and turned, trying to get back to sleep. But every time he closed his eyes, he saw monsters—terrifying monsters that wanted to hurt him and his sister. Hearing a scream, his body shuddered under the blankets. He sat bolt upright. He had to check on his sister. He had to make sure she was safe. Wrapping his dressing gown around him and pushing his feet in to nice warm slippers, he made his way along the corridor to where the screams were coming from. The candles in the walls were still burning, creating a line of jagged light. The long passageway echoed with the sound of pain. Something was wrong. He should have stayed with his sister. He shouldn't have left her alone. But Nurse should be with her, shouldn't she? He shuffled through the passage as the screams turned to sobs. The door of the nursery was just ahead. He stopped to take a breath and curled his small fist around the handle. He could almost see his heart beating through his velvet robe. Why is she crying so much and where is Mama? He strained to hear his mother's footsteps coming down the corridor. They didn't come. But he was the big brother. He had to protect his sister.

He pushed the door open. He saw the flicker of a candlelight over the crib. His baby was frantic. The maid was over her. And for the briefest moment, he felt relieved.

But Ariane looked up, and wild eyes flew at him. 'What are you doing here? You should be in bed.'

'I heard my sister screaming. Why is she screaming?'

He ran towards the crib. The knife flashed in the maid's hand. Ajeya's cheek was cut and bright red blood was running down her face. Cornelius cried out, but the maid's hand was over his mouth in an instant. The knife pierced his cheek.

'Don't you say a word, Cornelius. Don't you dare do anything stupid or this knife will do the same to you. Do you hear me?'

Despair howled in his head. His sister was screaming. He needed to pick her up and take her to his mother. But Ariane's knife wanted more blood.

'You did this, Cornelius. You did this to a baby. I came in and found you cutting your sister's face.'

He struggled to get free. He was squirming and trying to sound an alarm, but she was too strong for a three-year-old boy.

'Do you want me to do the same to you?'

He fought desperately to release her grip on his mouth. His words were lost in her clammy palms.

'That's right. I didn't think you did. Now I am going to let you go, and we are going to walk back to your room, nice and quietly. Is that clear?'

His muffled sounds were inaudible. The pain of not being able to protect his sister was immense.

She marched him back to his bedroom and closed the door just as the Emperor and his wife rushed past on their way to the nursery.

In his bedroom, she kept to her story that she had

found him hurting his sister. She had taken the knife off him just as he had woken from a trance. After months of saying it over and over to him, to the point where he pushed his knuckles into his mouth to muffle his cries, he finally believed that he had deliberately inflicted the wound. From that day on, he retreated to his room where he drew pictures of monsters and became afraid of the dark.

No one knew what happened that night. The maid told anyone that would listen that it was evil at work. She said it so many times to the Emperor that he believed it as well. He never looked at his daughter again.

THE ORB CONTINUED TO SWIRL—SHOWING a family in ruins. All happiness had frayed, and in its place came hate and fear.

THE EMPRESS WAS BANISHED to separate quarters for giving birth to a mutant. The maid told Eujena how she had caught Cornelius cutting his sister; and so, a thorough investigation was called off by Eujena for fear of losing her son.

Two years later, Eujena and her daughter were banished to the wilderness. Cornelius grew up believing he had inflicted the wound, and as a teenager, he continued to draw pictures, write poetry and play music, until he too was banished from the kingdom.

The Emperor continued his spiral to the depths of depravity. He would never find happiness again.

. . .

THE ORB STOPPED ROTATING. The group looked ashen. Ajeya was sobbing. Dainn was shaking his head in disbelief. Saskia held on to a trembling Cornelius.

'Why did she do it?' cried out Ajeya.

'Jealousy,' said Sansara. 'She was jealous of your family and jealous of you. She wanted to inflict as much pain and as much damage as she could.'

'Why, though, why? She destroyed our family. Look how everyone changed. I thought my father was a tyrant, but he wasn't. I thought he hated me, but he didn't. He loved me. He was a good husband. He was a good father. He was a good man before that monster changed him.' Ajeya was inconsolable. Look how the whole of the kingdom was affected by that one single act of malevolence. The loss of human lives, the torture that ensued, the wars that scarred the lands—all because of what she did to us and how it changed my father.'

'We know. We have seen. But the Fates will not let it go unpunished.' Sansara was solemn.

'Nothing can pay her back for what she did to us and to our kingdom.'

The group was sombre.

'Envy is a grotesque poison. It seeps into the hearts of men and turns them into monsters.' Dainn's rhetoric was grim.

Sansara response was even more shocking. 'I can tell you that... she drowned in the sea of Ataxata one night, just after you and your mother had left the palace. Her human body was never found. But I have seen what happened, and I know that the Fates have been waiting for this day.'

'I, too, have waited for this day.' Ajeya took her brother's hands. 'You were such a good brother to me. You even chose my name.' She brushed away the tear. 'And look, my totem is the hare. I was given it as a small child.' She showed him her tattoo and he traced the image with his finger.

Her vex continued. 'That monster tried to part us forever. But now that we have found each other, I will never be parted from you again.'

He held her close and kissed the top of her head. 'My beautiful sister—so precious and pure—who was always meant to be the hare.' He smiled at the memory of his drawing. 'Such a dreadful tragedy was bestowed on us. Our father loved us both. He loved our mother. How cruel our paths have been though the Fates have been seen to punish those that harmed us and has given both of us another chance.'

She wrapped her arms around him and lay her cheek against his breast. The pause was consuming as brother and sister united again. A myriad of emotions flowed through their veins as they both came to terms with the past.

'You must take up the position at the Palace at Ataxata,' Cornelius said at last. 'You should rule with Dainn. You have remained pure and without blemish throughout your life. Dainn is a valiant leader. It is you who should be crowned ruler of Ataxata with Dainn at your side.'

'But Cornelius. It is your birthright.' She stepped back in shock.

'No, Ajeya. It is your birthright. I may have been the first born, but you have earned the right to the throne.'

Her face creased into a frown.

'I haven't acted wisely. I put my own feelings before my subjects. I lost the right to rule years ago.'

'But you have made amends, Cornelius. You have repented and know the error of your ways.'

He shook his head. 'It's not enough to be a ruler.'

Her frown softened and she took his hands in her own. 'I don't know what to say, brother, because this is most gracious of you. But I will only take up the post if you promise me one thing.'

'Anything.'

'That my home will always be your home and that we will visit each other regularly.'

'I would be heartbroken if we didn't.'

She hugged him again.

Sansara spoke more solemnly.

'Your bond is limitless. Your love is strong. But our quest isn't over yet. The fates are still at work and we must be on our way.

CHAPTER TWENTY-SIX

The path they took was hazy, though the day was free from rain. The journey shouldn't take them long at this time of year, but a swirling fog descended quickly and became particularly dense and unnerving. The dragon moved through it carefully. The party held on tightly.

'I don't like this at all,' said Ajeya in a whisper. 'It feels like all the wraiths of hell are watching us.'

'I know. I feel it too,' said Dainn.

The air was sharp and cold now and brimming with screams of terror. Sansara felt the fear trembling through the others, and she urged her dragon to accelerate. Still the fog clung to them, damp and cold and eerie. They flew past misshapen objects spiralling out of the swirl: axes, bayonets, swords and daggers wet with blood and glistening with fear. Beyond that, churning through the mist, came the shrieks of headless ghouls and skeletons wielding bloodied weapons chasing after them. Then the fog became more dense, and out of the brume, disfigured corpses bearing rotten gums were feeding on ribbons of flesh and tendrils of sinew.

'What is this?' said Ajeya, leaning into Sansara.

'This is Ariane's world.'

'Can you do something?'

'I am not permitted. The Fates are at work here.'

'I'm sure there's something behind us,' cried out Cornelius from the rear.

Saskia followed his gaze and peered towards the mist. 'I can't see anything.'

'I know, that's what I'm afraid of. The mist is concealing it. But I'm telling you, something is out there, and it's getting far too close.'

Dainn unsheathed his sword. Ajeya strung a bow.

'Those weapons cannot help us, but I admire your bravery and tenacity.' Sansara gripped the staff at her side. The dragon soared ahead.

THE SMELL CAME FIRST. Its breath was a sickening over-powering odour of death, rot, and decay. Four enormous heads protruded from the body of a frenzied serpent, each one bearing wide split jaws of venom, each one-eyed head maddened with malevolence. The fiend had no claws or thunderous legs, only a grotesque, gelatinous body, born from the depths of the ocean, raging in a frenzied feast. The four heads reared at the dragon's tail, projecting their poison. Each mouth jostled for a body to devour.

'What is this evil?' cried out Ajeya. She launched a tirade of arrows, each one dodged by the writhing heads.

'That is Ariane. This is her fate.'

'And we have to fight her?'

'You do. You all do.'

'That monster will take more than a few battle weapons to slay it,' said Dainn, witheringly. 'We must go faster.'

The dragon accelerated, weaving through the trees and launching itself high over the clouds. The four heads were still on its tail, weaving faster in anticipation with long strands of hungry drool swinging from its jaws. The grey body sagged in the mist, gelatinous and huge, writhing in a hideous grey blur. The jaws were close now, long sharp teeth snapped wildly as they attempted to take on the might of the dragon.

'That thing is going to get me. She's fuelled with loathing and hate.' Cornelius' angst reached the ears of Sansara.

She gave a command to the dragon who turned mid-flight. Rising higher still, and standing on its tail, it torched the serpent with red hot flames of fire.

'Spot on,' cried out Cornelius. 'You got her first time.'

'Don't be too quick to breathe just yet.' Dainn's voice was grim. 'There's a lot of evil in that thing to conquer.'

The dragon waited. It was ready with another blast. Its cargo desperately hanging on, each one hardly daring to breathe.

Then it came again.

Through the flames it launched towards them.

The ordeal was far from over. Again, the dragon

stood tall and roared from the depths of its belly. The fire engulfed the serpent, drowning it in fire.

Cornelius spun around. He couldn't believe that the ogre had been disabled. 'She's gone, she's not there anymore.' He swivelled his head from side to side, over his shoulder—looking for a sign or a whiff of the smell.

She rose up from beneath and a head grabbed Cornelius. His voice for help was lost in the mist. Saskia and Ajeya screamed.

'Not again!' cried out Saskia. 'Hasn't he been through enough?'

'The Fates decide all, but I'm not going to give up.' Sansara gave another command to her dragon. It turned again, ready with another blast. But the monster was too dangerous. One of the heads had Cornelius in a firm grasp.

'I can't do anything. He is not immortal now. My dragon is too powerful. She might take him out as well.' Sansara shouted out what the party already knew.

'There must be something we can do.' Ajeya fired off another round of arrows. The heads dodged most of them, but the last one impaled in the beast's neck. It roared in anger, trying to remove it. It had no chance. Ajeya was out of arrows now. She roared back at the beast. 'You destroyed my father and you tried to destroy me and my brother. But I am a warrior, and I will have my revenge.'

Dainn threw his sword into the open mouth of one of the heads. Its snapping jaw rolled off its neck, the sword going with it.

Saskia threw her dagger into one of the eyes. Warm

blood spurted black over Cornelius. The beast was disabled, but they were out of weapons now. And still two heads were fighting over the squirming body of Cornelius while he kicked and punched for all he was worth.

Time was ticking by.

Time they didn't have.

Then, through the mists, they saw it. Coming up in the distance was the red dragon. The two fighting heads didn't see it. They couldn't detect it. The incoming predator was silent and swift in its attack, and as it snapped the serpent in two with its massive great jaw, Cornelius was flung to the ground. The blue dragon swept down to save him from the fall, and now Sansara could use the staff and project her invincible wrath. With a voluminous glow from her weapon, the serpent was incinerated to a pile of ashes. This fiend would rise no more. This evil had finally been terminated.

'Now doesn't that feel good, Ajeya. You got to witness the fate of Ariane.' Dainn was triumphant.

'Yes, it does feel good, though best of all is the knowledge that the last two faces she ever saw was mine and my brother's.

Cornelius was back in his place behind Saskia. The red dragon escorted them to their destination.

'You may not be immortal anymore, but you certainly have some awesome guardians looking after you.'

Cornelius smiled and leaned into Saskia. 'I know, I thought I was a goner back there. But hey, I am lucky to have a sorceress with a couple of dragons as daughter.'

'You certainly are.'

Dainn looked round and grimaced. 'That black blood is putrid.'

Cornelius looked down at his apparel and tried to wipe away the stench.

'Don't worry about small incidentals like that, Father. I can sort it out once we are safely on the ground.' Sansara's retort from the front was quietly settling for everyone.

CHAPTER TWENTY-SEVEN

The party had covered some considerable distance now, and the wrath of their encounter was soon put to rest. It was late afternoon when the dragons began to circle a wide perimeter before their descent, and all on board knew that they had reached their destination.

Seeking the perfect location, the dragons hovered in the air and waited as Sansara released the gnarled wand to the ground. And as the travellers watched from their safe distance, a fortress grew from the old withered stick. First, a crescent of dark stone formed a huge impregnable wall that soared from the land like a miniature mountain with turrets and towers growing tall against the afternoon sky. Then a gravel walkway appeared, dominating the front of the fortress with two lookout towers on either side of a heavily engraved gate. A new citadel formed the centrepiece, and with a magnificent spire that disappeared way into the clouds, it promised to be the grandest in the land. Beyond the curtain wall there appeared to be more than one hundred hectares of animal grazing land, complete with its own tannery, storerooms and outbuildings, while within the wall was a town for about five thousand inhabitants or more. Its crenellated outer walls stood thirty feet high, with towers at each corner, and each one half again. From every turret and spire hung the banners of the House of Cornelius emblazoned with the insignia of the Blue and Red Dragons: two fire breathing beasts facing each other that commanded both respect and allegiance from those who ventured close to its proximity.

'My gift to you, Father,' said Sansara as the dragons circled to a halt inside the enclosure. The party disembarked. Sansara just had one more thing to do, and instantly the terraced lawns were being prepared for a wedding.

The red dragon came over and with a gentle necking action, caressed the bigger blue beast, then reducing their size, they took up their positions on two giant pillars outside the gates of the castle.

'What is this, daughter?' Cornelius looked in awe at the fortress around him.

'It's my wedding gift to you both. You and Saskia will be married here today.' She gestured with her hand. 'And all of this is now your home.'

'I am speechless. This is more than I could ever have imagined.' Cornelius was still taking in the spectacle when Sansara added another piece of important information.

'Coben and Moira will be joining you today. They will also be married here... with you... in a double wedding.'

'You saved Coben?' Saskia beamed.

'Yes, the Fates decided that he should be saved. He is a good man who didn't deserve to die. He saved a lot of people, so he was granted his request.'

'I cannot thank you enough.'

'He has been with his daughter, Lace, catching up and spending time with her. They had a lot of talking to do. He has told her about you, Saskia, and how you reminded him of his Lace.'

Saskia wiped the warm tear with the back of her hand. 'Great goddess from the sky, you have helped so many people. We are indebted to you.'

'I hope that I, too, am rewarded when I go back home.'

'What?' Cornelius spun round. 'You are not staying here with us?'

'No, dear father. I have another life in another world. I cannot stay, I am not permitted to. But you can always call me. I will always be able to hear you.'

'How long do we have with you?' Saskia asked.

'I will stay till the sun goes down on this day. Then I have to return to my island.'

Cornelius and Saskia had to relent, and with heavy hearts, they nodded their heads and accepted that it was her destiny.

THE CLOCK STRUCK four and Sansara knew it was time. She gave an order and the huge oak gates slowly opened. With an outstretched hand, she gestured towards the thousands of guests who were arriving by any means of transport that they could.

'These are your friends, Cornelius. There will be many here that have crossed your path. You will recognise them all.'

'All of them?'

'Yes, all of them. See, over there is King Lyall and his wife Arneb arriving with King Namir and Skyrah. Gya and Macus and all those at the Clan of the Mountain Lion are greeting the residents of the Smilodon Fort. There are Torré and Lace with the rest of the Marshland Tribe. Siri from the Giant's Claw is here with his brother Zeno and his wife Colletti. Over there are all the prisoners from Hezekiah Hall, including your father and mother, Saskia. They are surrounded by those at Condor Vale. Squire Dom and Asher have recently married, so they are chatting with Tiller and Winta, who have also wed. So many friends have come to witness your marriage and celebrate this joining of kingdoms.'

'It's amazing, truly amazing. Look, Saskia, those are the men I was imprisoned with.'

Sir Laus was standing there, tall and dignified with the air of nobility—a handsome man of impeccable character. His father had served King Canagan at Castle Dru but had fallen during the siege five years ago. Sir Laus now resided at Sturt Manor, north of the castle, but still had links with King Lyall and his brother. Will stood next to him, sharing a joke and supping on ale. Nate had travelled twenty miles to be there on this memorable day—his fishery had been dredged and refilled with trout and carp. Fyn's herd of Red Hereford cattle survived, and his ruddy skin and sparkling eyes shone out like jewels. Identical twins, Jak and Ike, owned a vast tree plantation, east of Break Pass Ridge. They had also built their empire back up again.

Tion the blacksmith was laughing alongside them, and Lord Eryk from Condor Vale was in attendance with his wife, Lady Matilda, and their son, Viscount Mattius.

But then, quite possibly, the most important person of the day appeared, making her way through the dense throng. Looking dwarfed and frail, Sansara paved a path of gold and lifted her up to a higher level and guided her towards the front.

Ajeya's eyes lit up and she held her hands out as Sansara gently settled the elderly woman on the ground. Ajeya wreathed her arms round her mother's neck and breathed in the scent of familiarity. The moment took her back to when she was a small child. She stood back and looked into her mother's eyes.

Eujena reached out, and with a gentle finger, traced the flawless skin. She smiled at the girl who looked back at her.

'Your face. The mark. How is it possible?'

Ajeya looked at her niece. 'Sansara did it, Mother. She took it away.'

Eujena turned to look at her grandchild with searching eyes.

'I will explain all later, my dear lady. It will all become clear to you then. But for now, you need to speak to your children, but I will show you the events after the wedding.'

'She will, Mother,' said Ajeya. 'It will all become clear.'

Eujena nodded in agreement and turned to her

daughter. 'You always were beautiful and strong. The scar has defined you, but I'm glad it has gone now. Perhaps you needed to know the truth for it to vanish.'

Ajeya looked at Sansara and smiled.

So you know the truth now?'

'Yes, I do, Mother.'

'And can you forgive him?'

'Him? You still think it was Cornelius? You are wrong, Mother. It was the maid. It was Ariane.'

Jena's hands flew up to her face. 'No! No! Please tell me that it isn't true.'

'Yes, Mother, it is true.'

'But she told me it was Cornelius. She told me to stop the inquiries. She said that if I didn't back down, the investigators would discover he did it and take him away from me.' A spear could have ripped through her heart and she would have felt less pain. 'I have lived with that story for years. I didn't want to believe it then, but now my trust in another, over my own son, has come back to haunt me.'

'Mother, it is not your fault. It was very calculated. Even Cornelius believed that he had inflicted the wound. She said it so often to him. We also believe that she fed her poison to the Emperor, forcing him to get rid of me so no more questions would be asked.'

Eujena looked mortified. 'But why did she do it in the first place?'

'Jealousy, that most wretched of vices.'

'And I left him with her...' Eujena's vision went white as her mind raced back to the dreadful time.

'Yes, he has been through many bad times, and he

also has the mental scars to prove it. But he has come through it, and if you turn around, you will see what a fine man he has become.'

Eujena turned to face the son she hadn't seen for over twenty years. Tears welled in her eyes and she held out her arms to embrace him.

The entire congregation stood still around them. Ajeya could not curtail the weep. She stood between Dainn and Sansara as mother and son were at last reunited.

Eujena held him close for the longest time. She didn't want to let him go. He couldn't let her go either, but he wanted to look at her and stepped back to behold her ageing beauty.

'Mother, at last, I can't believe this day has come.' He held her hands.

'Cornelius, I have worried about you for so many years. And now here we are, united in front of all these people, with Ajeya and Dainn, and now you are to be married.'

He smiled and wiped away the tear.

'No mother could be more proud than I am this very day. To be reunited like this is more than I could ever wish for.'

'Mother,' he held her hands. 'I didn't have a good start in life. With Ariane terrifying me, and then my father, and the General. It's little wonder I became corrupted. But I am the person I am today because of the goodness in your heart. I was born a good person. I have been helped by all these people who stand before us. ' He turned to view the throng. He nodded to Namir and

Lyall, to Gya and Macus, to Torré and Lace. 'And now I stand with my mother, my sister, my daughter and my future wife, and I am testament that good does prevail, and peace can resume in our kingdoms.'

'Hear, hear to that,' echoed Lord Eryk, and a round of applause ensued around the pavilion.

Everyone who passed through the gates came to shake his hand, to embrace him and wish him well. He was bestowed with so many gifts that the gestures went on for the longest time. The importance of the day pressed in on Sansara. She signalled to two waiting attendants to escort Saskia and Moira to their bridal apartments. Cornelius and Coben were ushered into a separate room. Everyone knew that the stage was set for the celebration to continue in the grandest way possible.

CHAPTER TWENTY-EIGHT

Saskia's apartment was particularly splendid and the fragrance of aromatic petals and essential oils wafted round the room. A deep enamel tub, standing on four enormous claw feet, was a pristine white. With two ornate gold taps in the shape of fire breathing dragons, it bubbled in the corner as it was being filled. She looked out of the window, and from her high elevation, stretching out before her, lay the magnificent grounds of Dragons Spire.

The glow from the sun dappled the grass a sheen of silver, and the jewelled spire of the citadel shone like a beacon reaching up to the sky. Laughter echoed through the corridors. Outside, thousands of friends and acquaintances dotted around the enclosure , milling around, telling jokes, sharing experiences, and engaging in deep conversation. Nothing could be more perfect on her wedding day, she thought.

She watched for a while before casting an eye around her spacious dressing room. Sparse in the way of furniture, the carved marble walls intrigued her with more golden inlays of dragons, wild beasts, and mythical figures. The domed ceiling reached up to the rafters and resembled a twilight evening with a myriad of stars. She went back to the bath and turned off the taps. As she shrugged out of her robe, it pooled on the polished marble floor like a whisper. Stepping into the water, the pungent oils separated, and the petals rushed to her skin. Sinking down, she let the water run over her body and she breathed in the sweetest aroma of cinnamon, rose water, honey, and hyacinth. She closed her eyes and leaned her head back against the roll of the lip.

A sigh eased out of her, and the warmth settled into her thoughts and body, melting away all the stresses of the past few days. She felt instantly relaxed. She thought of Vlavos and spoke to him in a soft voice. *How far I have come, dear brother. What a journey I have been on. How much I have learned. And now look at me, released from the prison in my ivory tower, to all of this. To marry a man whom I love deeply. This is everything I have ever wished for.* She saw his face, smiling and happy for her, and he reached to out to cup her face. She closed her eyes and held him there. He could now relax, she thought. He did not have to stand guard over her anymore. He could be a valiant knight in his new dimension. She felt his touch melt away. She opened her eyes and reached out for him, but his fingertips were just a breath away. The drips from her fingers rippled in the bath water, creating swirls amongst the delicate frangipani petals. But he had gone. But he would never be far from her thoughts. Not ever.

She then reflected on Moira and Coben. She couldn't

wait to see her again. To see her married to Coben was more than a dream come true. Vlavos would be pleased for them both.

She noticed that a small glass of lemon water had been left on a porcelain table within easy reach. When she held the delicate vessel to her lips, she sipped from it slowly, letting the liquid swill round her mouth before letting it slide down her throat.

Two serving girls came in with plump clean towels, jewels, and accessories while another carried her bridal gown over two outstretched arms. They busied themselves arranging the bridal attire while Saskia dried herself in front of a full-length gilt-edge mirror. The girls lead her into the dressing area and provided her a chair in front of a long marble table. On the table lay an assortment of combs and brushes, powders and perfume bottles. And as her hand lightly touched the exquisite array of jewels, she was invited to sit down while her hair was brushed and curled so it fell down her back in soft ringlets. Pearls were clipped to her ear lobes, and a necklace was secured round her small neck. And as she eased into her bridal gown and slippers, she heard the call below for the guests to make their way to the wedding pavilion.

MOIRA SLIPPED into her boudoir and closed the door behind her. The room was adorned with a soft weave pale blue carpet, and tall vases of hyacinth filled the air with a rich aroma. She clasped her hands beneath her chin and turned in a slow circle, absorbing every detail. 'I cannot believe this,' she whispered, 'I truly cannot believe this.' The walls were panelled in pink alabaster and flecked with gold leaf. The bed was like a sleigh with richly embroidered furnishings and pillows plumped up high, one on top of the other. She wanted to launch herself on it but decided that she and Coben should share that moment together. An enormous white mirror was propped up against a wall and the chandelier above it sent spectrums of light across the room. She opened a wardrobe and a cloud of frankincense wafted from the gowns hanging there. She knew that she had to choose one dress. They were all beautiful, but her eye was attracted to a particular shade. She took it out, and hanging it on the wardrobe door, stood back to admire it. Then she heard the sound of running water and found a maid drawing her a bath. A privacy divider allowed her to change into a robe, and she waited on a deep seat set into a large bay window. It was piled with cushions and the windowsill displayed scented candles. And as the taps tapered to a gentle drip, the maid left her alone with her thoughts.

'I hope you can see us, dear Vlavos. I hope you can see how happy your sister is today. And whilst I may be marrying the man who trespassed on our land and led those soldiers to commit a dreadful sin against all of us, he did honour your death. I hope you can see the good in him like the rest of us do. We all miss you, my darling boy. We all love you, so very much. But I know you will always be with us, just as you have been during all those dark days that we encountered.' She felt a breeze curl around her neck. A soft kiss landed on her cheek. And she knew that she had his blessing.

THE HUGE HALLWAY was tiled in marble and in the centre a massive staircase led up to the first floor rooms and beyond. At the top, the ceiling was painted with landscapes of seas, mountains, and meadows. A feeling of flight and supremacy ensued.

Downstairs, one of the rooms led into the Dragons' Hall, an imposing room of immense character and wealth. The walls were gold stuccoed with dragons coiled around several ornate niches. Its roof was lapis and curved into a dome where huge nuggets of silver shone out like stars. Several sofas and armchairs were arranged on a plush blue carpet. A tray of tea had been left for the two men. The maid bowed low as she made her exit. The men took their seats.

'Well, Coben, it is good to meet you at long last,' said Cornelius, raising a cup to him. 'We never got much of a chance to chat.'

Coben smiled. 'No, we didn't. They were very difficult times for everyone. But because of you, all those who should have been saved that day have lived to tell the tale.' He sipped his tea like an astute gentleman.

Cornelius swallowed his and licked his lips with the satisfying taste. 'There were a lot of people involved in the dramatic escape. You teaching Saskia, listening to Philipe, helping Tiller. My daughter may not have been able to do all of it. I think she was able to assist because the Fates saw the determination in all of us and how each one of us would not give up. They saw how we overcame those hardships.'

Coben nodded. 'Yes, I certainly am a changed man. And I have four women to thank for that.'

Cornelius raised an eyebrow in response.

'Saskia and Moira, my daughter Lace, and your daughter Sansara.'

Cornelius nodded with pride and pursed his lips into a smile. 'I am so glad that you have been reunited with your daughter and met her valiant husband, Torré. Today you will wed Moira. The Fates knew you had repented your sins and have rewarded you handsomely for it.'

'And you, too, dear man. Look how far you have come. You have rekindled your relationship with your sister and given her the Palace of Ataxata. What a generous offer that was. And now you are to reside in Dragons Spire with my ward, Saskia.' Coben leaned back to take in the spectacle of the jewel-encrusted room.

'I would not have made a good leader, Coben. I still have much to learn. I sometimes think women make for better rulers. Don't you?'

Coben pushed out a laugh through his nose as he thought of the strong women he had met. 'You are not wrong there, Cornelius. Us menfolk still have a lot to learn.'

They clinked their cups by way of an agreement. Their laughter bounced off the pillars.

'You must come here whenever you wish.' said Cornelius. His laughter lines remained in place. 'You will always be welcome. You know that, don't you? Saskia has made it very clear that this is your home whenever you need it.'

'Thank you, Cornelius, and I will be sure to thank Saskia. And, of course, we shall take you up on your offer from time to time. Philipe has offered me work on the estate of Aiden Hall, and I know that Moira is still keen to work there and serve the Mistress Nolene.'

Cornelius nodded in agreement. 'Well, the distance is not far, dear friend. All of us in the Kingdom of Durundal are in close proximity, so thrice yearly celebrations should herald our continued peace and unity.'

'And one of those celebrations will be to mark our freedom, on this very day, every year. Have you seen how all the former captives of Hezekiah Hall are free of their **H** brand now?'

Cornelius looked at his own wrist. 'Freedom at last, and peace prevails throughout the kingdoms.'

'Hear! Hear!' rejoiced Coben. He finished his tea just as the announcement filtered through the windows.

'I think we are about to share our most important day,' said Cornelius, hearing the call.

'I think so, too,' said Coben. 'Come, dear friend, let us go and meet our brides.'

CHAPTER TWENTY-NINE

'Ladies and gentlemen, please, if you could all take your seats, I think we have a double wedding to enjoy.' Sansara instructed the ushers to show the guests to their seats, and as she stood at the back watching the proceedings, she sent a thousand white doves into the sky and carpeted the ground with fragrant frangipani petals.

Cornelius and Coben entered by way of a huge trellised construction where more jasmine and fragrant honeysuckle could be seen wrapped around the ornate maroon and turquoise carved pillars. Sunlight bounced off glass vases ablaze with the rich vibrant colours of a summer's day. And intricate paint work weaved in patterns of gold-edged flowers lit up the rows of chairs assembled round the pavilion.

The congregation were now seated in tall chairs with carved arms that took the shape of dragon's claws, and Meric stood at the altar waiting for the bridal party at the end of a very long aisle. Cornelius and Coben walked slowly down the golden path where they acknowledged those people furthest away with a wave and shook the hands of those that were nearest to them. Cornelius looked regal in a weaved tunic of muted golds and reds bound with a decorative sash made from the most luxurious blue satin. He bore the dragon insignia on his breast, and a scabbard with the hilt of a golden dragon hung loose from his waist. Coben wore the attire of a soldier, with a woven purple doublet and a sword at his side. His boots of black polished leather shone like tarred menhirs, and a medal of honour glinted on his breast. They were preceded by Troubador and Digger who dazzled everyone with diamond-encrusted collars bearing the newly carved wedding rings. And upon reaching the end of the aisle, the men took their places on double thrones of gilded oak, with the obedient dogs at their sides.

Here they faced their audience. In the front row sat Eujena and Hagen, flanked by Ajeya and Dainn on one side and Gya and Macus on the other. Next to Macus were Namir and Skyrah with their twin daughters, then Lyall and Arneb with their twin boys. Next to Ajeya sat Lace and Torré, then Zeno and Colletti, then Siri and Chay with Red and Rufus. Further spaces were reserved for two very important members of the bridal party who would take up their positions in a few moments. Behind them sat the former prisoners from Hezekiah Hall and all their families; and behind them, all the clans in the kingdoms. With the sound of a drum beating softly and a hushed flute chanting melancholy in the background, they chatted amongst themselves, sharing experiences and divulging new hopes for the future.

The two men spent a few moments taking in the ambience and sat quietly immersed in private conversation with each other. Then, as if by magic, all chatter was interrupted by a gasp from the congregation and they knew that there was nothing more elegant in the room. Everyone stood up at the sound of the fanfare. Saskia and Moira had arrived with Philipe to escort them to their grooms. He turned to each of them in turn and shared a smile as they began the long walk to take their places at the end of the aisle. Meric stood there, his eyes as bright as the path, reflecting the spectacle before him.

The women both wore dresses of ivory samite lined with a silver satin. Moira's was a lose bodice and a full skirt. Layers of expensive lace puffed out the creation and a blue, silk shawl hung delicately around her shoulders. Her greying hair was scooped up in loose curls and she wore a single blue orchid in the side. Her hands clasped a bouquet of forget-me-nots entwined with the pale blue gossamer of delphiniums, and she wore the subtlest fragrance with a hint of hyacinth.

Saskia's stunning ebony locks shimmered against the red thread in her dress. The material clung to every curve and emphasised her magnificent shape. The moth brooch that she always displayed was worn as a pendant which complemented her elegance and sent spectrums of brilliance across the pavilion. She wore a garland of scarlet posies in her hair and held a spray of red roses secured with a crimson braid. Her fragrance was one with a hint of rose oil which blended in lightly with the bouquet she carried. Behind them followed Nolene in a blushed rose, silk satin robe with her dark hair secured at the nape of her neck with an ivory comb and adorned with translucent pearls. She scattered fresh petals of red and blue roses where the bride's soft doeskin slippers skimmed the grass.

The music stopped as they reached Meric. Both men looked upon their women with pride. Cornelius thought his heart had missed several beats, while Coben had momentarily held his breath.

Both couples took their places on the ornate thrones facing their guests. Nolene took the bouquets and sat in the reserved seats with Philipe. Their fingers knitted together, and he placed a kiss on her cheek. The hushed audience eagerly anticipated Meric's words.

'Honoured guests and fellow countrymen, I am so very privileged and honoured to welcome everyone here to witness a very extraordinary but beautiful union of these people into the special bond of marriage. And to perform this union inside this magnificent pavilion fills me with immense happiness, pride, and exultation.'

Nods and hushed whispers echoed round the grounds.

'A wedding such as this, where the betrothed met each other under the most dreadful of circumstances, is a joy to behold, and we thank the gods that Saskia and Cornelius and Moira and Coben were destined to meet each other. We pray that they will live a long and happy life together.'

The couples acknowledged Meric as he continued. 'Marriage means so many things to different people, so I ask Coben to speak first and tell his bride why he has chosen her to become his wife.'

Coben and Moira stood up and taking Moira's hand, Coben spoke with love and affection. 'Once in a while, right in the middle of an ordinary life, the Fates give us the person who will make their lives whole again. A person who will fill a void that had been empty for so long.' He took a deep breath in memory of his late wife and son. 'I have loved this woman for many years...and for those years, I waited for the day to ask her to marry me. However, during all that time of waiting, I knew that she was part of my soul—the woman who completes me. And I will continue to honour her, protect her, and love her with all my heart.'

He thought of his beautiful wife who had died at the hands of the General. She would be looking down on him now with a smile on her face and a glint in her eye. She would embrace this union and she would love Moira as much as he did. He felt the warmth in his heart and knew she would be happy for him. He kissed Moira's hands and lowered his gaze while she composed herself to offer her accolade.

'And Moira.' Meric looked at her with smiling eyes. 'Please, will you respond with your words of love for Coben.'

She had to wipe away a tear and sniff back the sting in her eye. She was such a fortunate woman, and the love in her soul was immeasurable. Taking a deep breath, she spoke from the heart. 'Coben, you know how much I love you. You know that you are my rock and that I was meant to find you. And though we have waited a long time for this day, nothing would have been different had we married all that time ago. In fact, it has made us stronger. I love you for enriching my life and making me a better person. I love you for giving me back my freedom and helping all those people escape the clutches of a madman. Those people are here today because of you... and I am so proud. I love you for being you, for your kind heart, for your passion, and because I know that no one could love me as much as you do.' She, too, kissed his hands and lowered her gaze to the floor.

Amidst the whispers of courage, bravery, and friend for life, Meric waited a moment for all the people Coben had freed to settle down again. Coben gestured to Moira to sit first, and he took her hand in his as they both looked on at Saskia and Cornelius with pride.

'And now, Cornelius, could you please share why you wish to take Saskia as your wife.'

Taking her hand, Cornelius invited his bride to face him. 'My beautiful Saskia, whom I feel I have known forever. The person who has changed me and helped me as I faced my demons and honoured those who sought to mistrust me. From the first time I met you, I knew there was something special about you—a warm, loving, beautiful girl who has shown me on so many occasions the true meaning of love. The woman who wears the sign of the moth but who has the heart of a lion. She will always have my respect and my devotion, and I know that I will love you forever.'

The congregation felt the warmth of his sincerity around the hall. Eujena wiped the tears from her cheeks, having wondered on so many occasions if he would find true love. Now she couldn't be happier. Gya took her hand, for she, too, felt the same emotion.

'And Saskia, if you could respond to Cornelius.'

She looked into his eyes and smiled. 'My strong, courageous Cornelius, who I have learned so much from. We are so in tune with each other that I can sense how you are feeling even when there are walls between us. We have shared so many experiences together, experiences that are stored in my heart forever. No one knows their true strength until they are forced to acknowledge it, and we have both found ours. We have grown together—we are as one. I want to have children with you. To share our knowledge and our love. To secure a dynasty that is made up of trust, loyalty, and respect. I trust you, Cornelius. I respect you and will always be loyal to you. And with every beat of my heart, I will love you forever.'

Meric's voice filled the auditorium again. 'Thank you, all of you. Those words are timeless and heartfelt. They support the tribute of why marriage is so special to those who love and want to share their devotion.'

After a few minutes of silence, and after allowing Cornelius and Saskia to take their seats again, Meric held out his hands to conduct the next part of the ceremony.

'Now I have to retrieve the rings from these two faithful hounds.' He took each ring in turn and blessed them. 'These rings are a symbol of your love. There is no beginning or end, love is everlasting and bound in these solid circles for ever.' He placed them on a velvet pouch and moved slowly along the line.

Sansara wiped away a tear as she felt the obsidian

band around her finger and remembered the words of her own intimate wedding.

The captive audience held their breath as each couple took their rings, kissed them and placed them on their betrothed's finger. Moira's ring displayed the image of a dog, her faithful friend for so many years, and one who brought her the news she had longed for. Coben had the falcon engraved to symbolise his freedom. Saskia looked at the fine workmanship of the moth on her band, epitomising change, determination, and everlasting. Cornelius' bore the image of the dragon for strength, intelligence, and valour.

Meric placed Moira's hands inside Coben's. 'And now, please declare the covenant of marriage.' He held their hands together as they proclaimed the vow as one.

'Today we pledge our love.

We swear by the soil and water and all that surrounds us.

We swear by the falcon and the dog that protect us.

We swear by the gods and the spirits who look down on us.

We swear by all those who are present. This is our word.'

They stepped back and allowed Saskia and Cornelius to step forward. Meric placed Saskia's hands inside Cornelius'. 'And now, will you two please declare the covenant of marriage.' He held their hands together as they proclaimed the vow as one.

'TODAY WE PLEDGE OUR LOVE.

We swear by the soil and water and all that surrounds us.

We swear by the moth and the dragon that protect us.

We swear by the gods and the spirits who look down on us.

We swear by all those who are present. This is our word.'

MERIC SMILED at the union and concluded the ceremony. 'In the presence of the gods and spirits and totems, and with all these people gathered here today, I now pronounce you both husband and wife. Go and enjoy the day with your friends, enjoy the occasion with your loved ones, and enjoy your lives as married couples.'

After Meric's final words, the newlyweds walked up the aisle to their new life together. The path led to the celebration green where a wedding feast was waiting. There were singers and musicians, jugglers and tumblers, and a group of painted minstrels.

Under the protection of the enclosed pavilion, the first few notes of the reed pipes began to shiver across the lawn and the guests formed an arch. The couples crouched through the dome amid the calls of well wishes and cheers. The women of the congregation picked up ribbons of pure silk and made circles around the two couples, entwining them and binding them as the material brushed against their bodies. Cornelius held Saskia's hand and pulled her closer into him; Coben led Moira, and together they paraded round the enclosure as the ribbons curled wildly and passionately, casting a rainbow of colour at every turn.

Children threw petals at them, the men threw coins at them, the drums beat like a hundred hearts, and the flutes whispered through the silks. And above the festival of love, the gong sounded its deep sonorous call, bursting into a wave of shrill tones which echoed across the pavilion. In the courtyard, the spit was turning and the cauldrons were simmering. The smell of freshly baked bread, pies, and cakes were wafting. Sweet aromatic fragrances of infused wine, of orange and ginger deserts, and of cinnamon and lemon cakes tantalised the tastebuds. And amid the raucous laughter of speeches, anecdotes, renditions and song, the bridal party celebrated until the early hours. Laughter rang against the pillars and the guests refilled their glasses with a never-ending flow of wine. And when it was time to sleep, those who couldn't make it back to their dwellings were happy to lay where they fell, under a canopy of stars and a bright full moon.

SANSARA TOOK Eujena to one side when she got a moment. 'You have followed a challenging path, Eujena, but sometimes we all have to accept our destiny to find our strength.'

Eujena took her hands and smiled. 'Life's journey is never easy. We all have mountains to climb and messages to learn. I know what you have done for my family and for the whole of the kingdom. I cannot thank you enough.'

Sansara smiled back with love in her heart. 'I need to tell you everything, Eujena, and whatever you hear now you must believe. I will tell you things that seem impossible and highly improbable. But remember that we live in a world where everything is decided by what we can see and what we touch. If we can't see it or we don't understand it, then we perceive that it doesn't exist. But it does exist, and what may seem impossible here, is in fact highly probable in another world.'

Eujena nodded. 'I have seen enough things in my lifetime to expect nothing but to accept everything. I will accept what you tell me now. And I promise you, I will believe.'

Sansara revealed everything to Eujena. From the moment Ajeya was born, to the present day at Dragons Spire. About how all those gathered in her son's new home were connected in some way. She watched the pain melt away from this woman, and she watched the burden lift from her shoulders. And as she watched Eujena go back to her children with peace in her heart and pride in her soul.

She knew then that her mission was complete.

Sansara took one last look at the happy couples forging lasting relationships with the people of the kingdoms. She felt a tug in her heart knowing that she had brought them all together. For these acts of friendships would secure peace throughout the lands—a peace that would last for generations. With a feeling of pride, she walked through the wicket gate to be reunited with her dragons. Summoning them to rise from their sentry positions, the dragons flapped their huge wings and roared. The obelisks instantly morphed into two magnificent replicas, standing several feet tall. Once aboard the blue dragon, they circled the entire complex once; then, turning on a recumbent leathery wing, she was transported back to another dimension.

CHAPTER THIRTY

THE DRAGONS SETTLED on the shore of Tarragon Island and nuzzled their faces into her warm embrace.

'Thank you for all your help. I could never have done this without you. You will come back and see me, won't you?' She didn't want to see them go. It was always painful to say goodbye.

They seemed to understand her dilemma, though. Sansara was sure that they could. Then the orb around her neck started to get larger and the constellation swirled. The Fates appeared in the mist and drew her in to speak to her.

'You have done well, Sansara, daughter of Mawi. You have made changes that will affect others for many lifetimes. You are a true warrior and crusader. You have earned the right to be a saviour. For it is written that a warrior will charge through the kingdoms and seek vengeance for those whom have been wronged. This warrior will be born from the seed of the living and the womb of the dead. Her name will be Sansara, her purpose will be to bring peace. She will be able to take many forms, but in this life, it will be of a human.'

The orb grew bigger still, bigger than anything she had seen before. It swirled and tumbled through the air.

'You have surpassed the prophecy, and now your work is done. But we did promise you something in return. And we will honour that promise.

'Raoul lives. Your child lives. His burned body was an illusion. The blood from your baby was where we delivered her. You would not have fulfilled the task with them in your thoughts. We had to anger you to see your true capabilities. We will not need to do that again. Go safely, Sansara, Sorceress of the Sapphire. When we need you again, we will call on you.'

THE ORB VANISHED. The dragons had gone. Her armour was replaced with a long red dress and a blue velvet cloak that pooled heavily at her feet. And on the top of the mound, she saw them: her husband holding Delphine in one arm and waving frantically to her with the other. Shielding her brow, she waved back to him before running up the path to where they waited.

The sound of birdsong from the forest was overwhelming, filling the air with a joyful return. Her heavy robe, embroidered with pure gold thread and countless shiny symbols, glittered in the diminishing sunlight as she ran towards him. She flew ahead, rustling the hedgerows, splashing through puddles, jumping over roots and burrows, gaining speed and closing the distance between them. Making her way up the hill, her haste was bursting, her throat ached with breath and spore. Her muscles were burning, her heart thundering, sprinting to the limits of her strength and beyond. She had only ever run this fast once before. But this time her heart and soul would not be wrenched from her core.

The cord was still pulling her in. Towards him. The distance between them was closing. And then she stood before him. Their eyes met and understanding flashed between them: the Fates had spoken true. Pilot and Porter stood with the yearling, the wolf family gathered between them. Raoul and Sansara were lost in a sea of emotions as he held out their new born for her to hold. She reached out to embrace her sleeping child for the first time. Tears and love flowed in quantities.

'I knew you'd come back.' His voice was shaky. 'The Fates said that you would return to me.'

She looked at her child adoringly, the bond was instant. She smiled back at him. 'The Fates said the same to me, my dearest Raoul. They told me that they had merely borrowed you.'

He wiped away the tears with the back of his hand.

'You were with me the entire time Raoul. I could feel you at my side, helping me through. I wouldn't have made it without you.'

Raoul took her hand and kissed it. The love in his eyes was immeasurable. He couldn't think of the right words—or he thought of too many words and they bunched up beneath his dry tongue.

But they both knew this was merely the beginning and all would change from this moment.

He held onto her hand and led her into their new

home where candles flickered in the window and the hearth crackled with warmth. The sun bowed out to the end of the day and the animals returned to their shelters where they hunkered down for the night.

IN MAWI'S KITCHEN, the crone awaited the return of her daughters. Phoebe was arranging the blue ribbon in her hair as she came through the door, and Ellis was tucking the red handkerchief into her sleeve.

Mawi's eyes shone brightly as they entered. 'Everything go as planned, daughters?'

'Oh, yes, Mother,' heralded Ellis. 'Phoebe was truly spectacular, and I got to sever the serpent maid in two.'

'Ellis really was quite splendid, and Sansara was magnificent—she really is the Sorceress of the Sapphire.' Phoebe beamed at her mother and sister.

'And the orb?'

'Of course, mother. Here it is as you requested.' Phoebe handed her the mineral.

Mawi took the stone in her old withered hands and felt the small pebble in her palms. It felt like any normal grain now. No one would ever know its true powers, she thought to herself.

SHE WENT to a large oak chest where a gold lacquered box was retrieved. The long ornate casket was trimmed with lapis lazuli and edged with sapphire stones. A heavy, gold amulet, crafted in the shape of a coiled sleeping dragon, lay atop the shiny smooth surface. Her fingers stroked the ancient artefact and found a delicately curved leverage, clasped securely to conceal the contents. Taking the key she wore around her neck, she unlocked the clasp to reveal a soft bedding of luxurious blue satin. Placing the stone carefully within its cocoon, Mawi closed the lid and waited for the soft click of the lever before locking it again and putting it back in the safe place.

'Rest now, dear Fates, for you have worked tirelessly on this mission. But I know it won't be long before you have another important task for us. Until such time—my daughters, Sansara, Phoebe, Ellis, and I, remain your loyal guardians.'

The End

'We are all connected.'

Meet S E Turner

S E Turner was born in the UK and currently lives 40 miles south of London. This is her first series, and there are at least another two being planned and outlined. Please follow her on Goodreads, BookBub and Instagram. And if you enjoyed the series, please leave a favourable review.

What inspired you to write The Kingdom of Durundal?

A visit to Scotland first inspired me. I found the wilderness to be breathtaking, the vast mountain ranges spectacular; and with its eerie atmosphere, you can almost hear the ancient clans talk on the wind. I climbed the great mound of Dunadd Fort in Kilmartin Glen; a royal power to the first Gaelic kings and home to a fortress some 2,000 years ago. From that vantage point I saw the far reaching views of the lochs, of castles, of caves and hidden grottos. I saw a story unfold before me. I saw pain and sorrow, love and comradeship, fear and courage. I saw the magic of a time gone by. I saw the Kingdom of Durundal.

As with all kingdoms where clans and courts live side by side; the realms of sacrifice and avarice are prevalent. That is the backbone of my series. Certainly by book 2: A Wolf in the Dark, the true depths to which those in power will go to is explored at some length.

Interestingly, from the first moment that Ajeya comes

riding in (A Hare in the Wilderness), to the part where Sansara returns to Tarragon Island (A Moth in the Flames), the timescale is only a few days. It's the history of the main characters that goes back some twenty five years; and it's that connection that holds the story together. And as is usual with folklore and ancient history; there has to be magic and dragons — hence the themes and characters in the final book.

How did you decide on the titles for your books?

When you write about ancient civilisations, albeit in a fantasy setting, there has to be a certain amount of research to keep it believable. Most of what you read about the clans is factual, and their totems are indeed very real. Our ancestors depended on them for safety, to please the spirits and to give the bearer added strength. I have tried to keep this bygone age alive in my books. The titles are the characters totems.

Your female protagonists are very strong. Why did you write them in?

Over the course of history there have been so many inspirational women, women of courage with a fire about them. I fear that sometimes women have lost that drive and ambition, and are portrayed as the weaker sex. I wanted to eradicate that belief and give all women a platform. A platform to shine, to be heard, and to give their very best. A platform to find their strength and make a difference. Think like Cleopatra, fight like Boadicea and live like a goddess.

Who is your favourite character?

I am asked that a lot, and I would have to say Cornelius. I think he had a bad start in life. He was the ultimate bad guy—he did some pretty awful stuff to Namir in: A Leopard in the Mist. He was a liar and a coward. But was it nature or nurture that made him that way? Whatever made him change, he came good in the end (A Stag in the Shadows). At that point I didn't know whether to kill him off or save him. I spent months considering the options. But in the end I decided to save him - because he is my favourite character. And to show that people can change— if they want to.

What would you say to a fledgling author?

Never give up on your dream. Read a lot of books in different genres, and write down all those little pockets of inspiration that pop into your head at the unlikeliest of moments.

S E Turner
www.kingdomofdurundal.com
www.amazon.com/author/seturner
www.instagram.com/sharon.e.t

Main Characters in the Kingdom of Durundal

CLANS

Clan of the Mountain Lion.
Laith - Leader
Artemisia - (Laith's childhood sweetheart)
Zoraster - medicine man
Namir
Lyall
Skyrah - Namir's wife
Arneb - Lyalls' wife
Meric - physician
Chay - Skyrah's mother

Clan boys:
Ronu, Bagwa, Norg, Suma, Targ,
Silva, Clebe, Hass, Wyn, Hali

Hill Fort Tribe
Colom - leader
Peira - Colom's wife
Jena - (Eujena, Empress of Ataxata)
Hagen - Jena's husband
Keao - Hagen's son
Red - Keao's wife
Rufus - Keao and Red's son
Ajeya - (Eujena's daughter)
Dainn - (married to Ajeya)

Clan boys:
   Storm, Durg, Malik, Tay

Clan of the Giants Claw
   Thorne - leader
   Ukaleq - Shaman
   Siri - 2nd leader
   Zeno - Siri's brother
   Colletti - Zeno's wife

Marshland Tribe
   Wargon - Leader
   Raven - Wargon's wife
   Torré
   Lace

Clan of the Smilodon
   Myra - Matriarch of Smilodon
   Gya - clan girl

COURTS

Castle Dru
   Canagan - King of Durundal
   Artemisia - Queen of Durundal
   Namir and Lyall - brothers
   Skyrah - Namir's wife
   Arneb - Lyalls' wife
   Meric - physician
   Chay - Skyrah's mother

MAIN CHARACTERS | 241

Palace in Ataxata
Emperor Gnaeus III
General Domitrius Corbulo
General Van Piers
Captain Vortim Vontiger
Captain Alverez
Cornelius Gnaeus IV
Marquis de Beauchamp
Macus - stable hand
Roma - maid
Scowler - guard
Poxface - guard
Ariane - maid

Hezekiah Hall
Segan Hezekiah - King of the mountain
Coben Hezekiah - brother/Captain of the Guard
Yurg - guard
Bryn - guard
Digger the terrier

Captives of Hezekiah Hall
Eryk of Condor Vale
Tion - blacksmith at Ataxata
Jak and Ike - brothers from Tree plantation.
Will - farmer at the old croft
Fyn - cattle rancher
Sir Laus of Sturt Manor
Nate - fish farmer at the lake
Squire Dom of Condor Vale

Aiden Hall

Philipe von Aiden
Nolene von Aiden
Vlavos von Aiden
Saskia von Aiden
Inga Smythe - pastor's wife
Moira - cook
Tiller - goat herder
Atilus - cow herder
Winta - kitchen maid
Asher - kitchen maid
Troubadour - family dog

Mawi Isand

Mawi
Phoebe
Ellis

Tarragon Island

Sansara
Raoul
Delphine
Pilot
Porter

I hope you have enjoyed the Kingdom of Durundal series. And if you want to continue reading my work, there is a brand new series to follow: The Sorceress of the Sapphire

Printed in Poland
by Amazon Fulfillment
Poland Sp. z o.o., Wrocław